A compilation of short stories

# 39 Emergency Exits

Stories by various 5photostory.com authors

Edited by J.D. Stamp

Copyright © 2006

All enquiries of any nature should be directed to the
publisher.

## ISBN 0-9550780-3-2
### 978-0-9550780-3-3

# First edition

## PUBLISHED 2006 BY 5photostory.com
## AN IMPRINT OF FYGLEAVES LTD
FYG STUDIO, WEST EALING, UK W13 9JR
www.5photostory.com          www.fygleaves.co.uk
COVER: WILLIAM RUSSELL © FYGLEAVES LTD
**Printed and bound by CPI Antony Rowe, Eastbourne**

# 39 Emergency Exits

## Contents

## Contributors

Tracie Barnett, Sharon Birch, Emilia Blain, Felicity Bloomfield, Lucy Brown, Caroline Carter, Catriona Child, Anuradha Choudry, Tracey Clues, S.E. Coldwell, Richard Crowhurst, Laura Dawn, Graeme Down, Swapna Dutta, Shelley Ellerbeck, Babette Gallard, Kate Greagsby, Sarah Ann Hall, Joss Hayes, Steve Jeanes, Dave Jobson, Lydia Jones, John Kent, Maggie Knight, Stephen Lake, Dan Lamb, A.J. Le Flahec, Brian Lockett, Jamie McGaw, Helen Meikle, Peter Morris, Nik Morton, Jackie Notman, Jenna Pogue, Samantha Priestley, Annette Reader, M.A. Rodger, William Simpson, Eleanor Smith, Rebecca Smith, Joanna Styles, Cally Taylor, Sylvia Telfer, Sarah Thompson, Naomi Walker, Halla Williams.

## Foreword

It has been a great pleasure, since the first Fygleaves competition in 2004, to read all of the many and varied stories which have been submitted. It has constantly been an amazement to see the wide variety of imaginative ideas weaved into and around the photos, and it is a tribute to the unique power of story-telling that so many stories, based on the same five pictures, can be so different.

As the judge of the competition, it has always been an agonising process to narrow down the entries in the short-listing stage, and I have always felt it a shame that the short-list fails to capture the full extent of the variety of stories submitted. When I discussed this with Fygleaves after the 2005 competition, we came up with the idea of this book – a compilation of the best and most imaginative entries from the 2006 competition. It is our hope therefore, not only that readers will enjoy the wide variety of settings, characters, and plots that the five pictures have inspired amongst so many talented and creative writers, but that these writers will find this book to be a springboard from which they can now aim higher, and let their imaginations roam even wider.

This is the aim of Fygleaves, to offer opportunities for new talent to break in past the barriers of the current publishing world: many of the writers entering our competition are previously unpublished, so it has been a delight to help enable them now to be authors revealing their leaves to the world, and I look forward to an even wider variety of imaginative talent being on display in 2007.

J. D. Stamp, 2006 (Judge D)

# 2006

An emergency exit

plus

a ladder, a key, a park bench and a petrol station

Steve Jeanes, Brighton


Storming The Citadel


"This is Jessica Melling. I can't pick up at the moment, but I so want to get your message. Please talk to me after the tone."

That's my girl. Even down a crackly phone line she sounded like she was purring and licking cream from my ear. I smiled.

"But if that's Ray, do me a favour, dear. I don't want to see you. Keep away from me, there's a good boy."

The smile felt suddenly stiff on my face. I took the receiver from my ear and stared at it then hit it hard, once, twice against its cradle.

The kid behind the counter looked up from his comic. I could tell he thought he should say something, but wasn't sure if I meant trouble. I put him out of his misery.

"Woman problems. Sorry about that."

His pitted landscape of a face nodded sadly. "Bad news, man. Chicks, huh? Hey, don't worry about the phone. Nobody uses it these days. Mobiles, yeah?"

"Yeah. Mobiles," I said, paying him for a Mars bar and twenty litres of diesel. "Only mine's broke. *She* did it."

"Bummer." He looked remarkably sympathetic for somebody with a lazy eye and a mouth full of gum.

"Yeah. Put a spiked heel right through the thing. No way that can be fixed. No way."

He shook his head wearily as he handed me a fist full of receipts, vouchers and special offers. "That's the pits. Anything I can do to help, like, you know, man."

Like, I knew all right. Knew I was in trouble – not how he could help. That was a ridiculous idea. The guy could hardly string two words together, let alone act as a mediator in a complicated relationship. And Jess and mine's was complicated up the wazoo. In terms of mediating difficulty, getting Israel and Iran together for a hog roast with free bar doesn't come close.

I also felt he might not have been well versed in the subtleties of love. Was it the way his little finger lingered in his left nostril as he returned to his comic? Or maybe the way his lips slowly followed the action? Who knows? I slipped out onto the forecourt and headed back to the Peugeot, my mind on other things.

So, Jessica didn't want to see me, eh? Well, I'm not the kind of man who takes no for an answer. Or even maybe. Faint heart never won blah blah. I floored the accelerator and headed for her flat. I knew she wouldn't be able to resist me face to face.

If I could get her face to face. Hunched in a solitary moonbeam outside Napier Mansions I must have appeared a desperate figure, patting my pockets with growing frustration. Would she really stoop this low, to go through my clothes and take my key without telling me? Yeah, she would. Behind that pussy-cat's purr there'd always lurked the snarl of a tiger, but taking my key seemed somehow beneath her. Petty and pointless. She knew well enough a little thing like a missing key wouldn't put me off. All I had to do was wait for another resident to use the front entrance and I'd be up the stairs to the third floor and storming the gates of her citadel.

Just one problem, there was no sign of anybody else using the door. I checked my watch. 3.38 am. It could be a long wait. Only, through the glass I could see the emergency exit door at the back. That gave me an idea. Maybe I could find a way to push the handle down. Something long and thin might do the trick. A wire coat-hanger, for instance. I grinned to myself. Maybe every cloud does have a silver lining, even when little gits rip off your car aerial. I retrieved its makeshift replacement and hurried to the rear of the flats, straightening the wire as I went.

Next problem, how to get it through? The door fitted tightly on all sides. Only at the top could I see any sort of gap. That would have to do then, but I'd need something to stand on. I looked around the back patio. Nothing of any use, or that I could move. A bike padlocked to the bike rack. A shed, also padlocked. Even the dustbins were chained to the back wall. And behind, it opened out into the communal gardens. There wouldn't be anything in there. Or would there?

I would have preferred something lighter, but after ten minutes of huffing and puffing, I'd dragged the park bench out from its resting place beneath the chestnuts and right up against the emergency exit door. Gold glinted along its spine – 'In Memoriam – Alfred Williams – 1926 - 2004 – He loved this park.'

"Sorry, Alfred, but needs must," I said as I stood on tiptoe on the back of the bench and fed the coat-hanger wire through the space at the top of the door.

Twenty minutes of frustrated fiddling around later, I gave up in despair. The wire went through the hole. I could even bend it so it reached down the door to the handle. But I couldn't get any pressure on the handle to spring the latch. I dropped down and squatted on the bench, then jumped up and barely suppressed a yell when I found myself sharing it with a bundle of stinking rags. The bundle of rags held a grime-rimmed bottle out to me. I declined the offer and made for the car. This was getting me nowhere.

I must have been sitting in the car looking up at her window for nearly an hour, and the hangover had begun to get a grip, when I ran out of ciggies. I rummaged through the glove compartment, desperately hoping for an abandoned packet, but finding only the stocking the stripper had draped over my head earlier that evening. A long ladder ran the length, and suddenly I had a plan. There'd been a ladder in the petrol station's forecourt, and that kid had offered to help, hadn't he?

It took my credit card as a deposit, but in the end he let me borrow it. In no time I was swinging my leg over the window sill and creeping across the bedroom.

Half way across, I heard the bed creak.

"Ray! What the hell!" A dark shape leapt from the bed.

I fumbled towards the switch.

"I'm turning the light on."

"No!" She screamed as she clapped her hand over mine. "No," she said again, more softly.

In the dark, she still looked beautiful, the soft curves of her face and body silhouetted by the moonlight. "OK," she whispered finally in that silky voice, "you can have your key back, but it's the settee for you. It's way past midnight and you *know* it's bad luck to see the bride before the wedding."

William Simpson, Broadstairs

## Chameleons

Chameleons fascinate me. The idea that they can merge into any background. Combining that camouflage with sex and weapons... The training for my occupation took place some time ago. But much of it seems like yesterday. Did I say occupation? It's a sideline nowadays. But it keeps me active.

I sat in the park. The only building overlooking it is the Sunnyside Residential Home. These days they call everything by a different name. Old folks are Senior Citizens. Foreigners are ethnic minorities. There was a time...

Memories. Mine were disturbed by the man who decided to join me. I looked him over. He was around a similar age. I recognised him.

"Hello, young Harold. Heard from George then?"

George is my nephew.

"Yeah. He said to give you this."

He handed me a folded newspaper. It had that feel of solid weight that they have nowadays, what with the colour supplement and all the rest. I was careful to let nothing fall out.

"George wants to know what day you're coming over."

"Did he say what day would be convenient?"

"He mentioned Thursday at eight."

"Thursday's tomorrow. It doesn't give me much time."

"I know. But – well, he's a bit busy."

I nodded in the slow and peaceful way people with

my experience tend to have.

"Thanks Harold. Tell him it's OK."

A young girl walked by, and I watched closely. Tight denim mini, cut low to expose the tattoo just above her arse. Harold's rheumy eyes swivelled. Fanciable, is little Caroline. She was Eileen's best mate at school, and now she's twenty-three, and in business. She didn't appear to notice us. It was amazing, the way we fitted into the background, like seals on a rock, or old folk on a park bench. Harold left, and I followed a few minutes later.

Back in my room overlooking the park, I opened the newspaper. The gun and silencer looked unused. Its thirteen round magazine was full. The key was there. Nothing written. George had covered all that on our last meet. Eight o'clock tomorrow.

My nephew is a touch old-fashioned. Some of his interests are not strictly legal. But then everyone's on the take nowadays. Iffy property deals in Bristol. Flogging off knighthoods to party financiers. There's an old Latin saying that begins *Quis Custodiet.* I can never remember the rest. It means that when the gaffers are bent, it's hard for the rest of us to go straight. But, as I said, George is old-fashioned. He doesn't touch drugs.

*No drugs on the manor,* is what he tells his slags. He had a daughter once. Eileen. Lovely girl. But she's dead. Of drugs. He knew the pusher's identity. So did the police and the council. But they wouldn't do anything. So my beloved grand niece, fifteen when she died, was to be avenged, and I was the one to pull the trigger.

Petrol Stations have changed. You can buy just about anything there, even petrol. They're respectable business locations. Good cover. The mark owned the station, and the offices above, from where the empire was run. An ideal set-up. Hundreds of cars coming by every day, stopping for five minutes, or ten at the most. In a short time those cars could be hundreds of miles away, some of them with more than petrol on board. That evening I crossed the park at my usual time, and went up the steps over the railway bridge. It's a goods line, and I'd checked the train times carefully. The petrol station was busy as usual. At five to eight, I entered, shuffling slowly as though stiff from a long car journey. There were loads of people standing in the queues. Nobody gave me a second glance. Once through the door marked 'Toilets', I slipped on thin rubber gloves, and pushed open another door marked 'EMERGENCY EXIT'. Out past the rubbish bins, and up a fire escape. The key fitted easily. I inched open the door.

The mark was at a desk, which was covered in money. There were sheaves of banknotes everywhere. A raised head, the mouth falling open in surprise. Then a patronising smile.

"Lost your way, dear? A bit confused? Don't worry, I'll take you down—"

I drew the gun, and the eyes widened, switching from my face to the death warrant of the muzzle. The two shots in the heart made no more noise than an old man coughing. The mark went over backwards. I checked. Mutton, dead mutton, lying half twisted to expose the bare midriff, and the tattoo just above her arse. The one who'd supplied her best mate with the ecstasy which had killed her, and who continued to make a living at it.

*"That's for Eileen, Caroline,"* I whispered. I relocked the door through which I'd entered, and dropped both bolt and chain on the main office door. Then across to the window, and through the roomy frame. The ladder was just where George had said it would be. I reached

through the louvers, managing to fasten the main window from the outside. The Bill would of course find it hadn't been locked. But by then that ladder would be long gone. Down the ladder, being careful not to slip, I headed for home via the bridge. There was a police mobile on the forecourt, the uniformed driver drinking coffee. They all look so young nowadays. He didn't even register my presence. Once on the bridge, I only had five minutes to wait, before a distant hooting announced the train, and its open coal trucks. It was soon gone, and the gun with it. Two minutes later the key was in the pond at the bottom of the rise, and three minutes after that, I was home.

Well, I call it home. It's not too bad. Sheltered accommodation depends a lot on the warden in charge, and our warden is pleasant. He knows who George is so maybe that helps. As I passed the reception desk I received a cheerful 'Goodnight love!" from the two nurses on duty. I caught the passing comments.

*Lovely girl... used to be in the SOE, so they reckoned... amazingly fit...*

Then I sat at the window, celebrating with a large brandy, and admiring the view. As I said, the Sunnyside Residential Home for Ladies overlooks the park, and the view is pleasant. In two days I'd fly out to meet George and close up the business end. An army pension doesn't go far, so a little earner is very welcome, three or four times a year. I finished the brandy, and looked at the bottle. Then I succumbed to temptation, and poured myself another. It went perfectly with a small Davidos.

I reviewed a successful operation. Occasionally I miss the old days, in occupied France. Old ladies, you know, are a bit like chameleons, practically invisible to anybody under fifty. There are some advantages in

16

*anno domini.* But I did lean forwards to close the window, which was producing a small draught. At seventy-nine, I always say, you can't be too careful.

Jackie Notman, Calne, Wiltshire

## The Job

"Right, now listen up everybody. We've got to make sure this all goes smoothly so we'll go over it one more time."

The gang groaned.

"Not again Micky boy."

"Yeah, we all know what we're supposed to do."

"Yeah, it'll be fine."

Micky shook his head. "One more time please gents." Micky was the biggest, and it was his plan, so they all agreed.

"OK. Ron, what are you gonna be doing?"

"I'm going to be at the petrol station keeping a lookout."

"Good man," Micky said. Ron looked pleased. "And what time you gonna be there?"

"About quarter to eight." Ron frowned. He wasn't sure that bit was right.

"It's '19:45 hours'," Micky sighed.

"Oh." Ron nodded. "What time's that then?"

Micky sighed again. He'd been doing a lot of that recently. "It's a quarter to eight Ron."

Ron smiled. Now he knew what was happening.

"And what will you be doing at the petrol station?"

"I'll be keeping a lookout."

"Good. And where will you keep a lookout from?"

Ron frowned again. "At the petrol station?" he asked.

"Yes Ron," Micky ran a large hand over his equally large face. "I meant, where in the petrol station will you be?"

"Oh." Light dawned for Ron. "Round the back, by the emergency exit."

"Good, because you can see them coming but they won't see you."

Ron nodded again. Micky looked round at the others. "That's the important bit. This has got to be a total surprise. You all keep schtum when you leave here."

The others nodded.

"Right. Davy," Micky continued, "what have you got to do?"

Davy was the youngest. He folded his arms and looked up at the ceiling. "I'm setting it up."

"Have you got everything you need now?"

"Yeah." Davy stretched. "I've just got to pick up the ladder but I'll do that tomorrow."

"And they won't find out?"

"Nah, I told 'em I was using it for a painting job."

"What time you gonna start?"

"19:00 hours Sir." Davy made a mock salute and giggled, looking at the others for encouragement.

"Stop taking the piss or I'll cuff ya," Micky growled.

"Right," Micky continued. "I'm taking care of party one and you Al have got party two." He nodded at the last member of the team.

"No probs Guv," Al replied. "Ten to eight, um, sorry, er 19," Al counted on his fingers, "50, I pick up party two and make for the—"

"Rendezvous," Micky cut in. "OK Davy, when you're happy that everything's set up and working then go along to Mum's place, you know where she keeps the key, and get the stuff OK? And Ron, you follow up from behind when we've passed you."

They all nodded.

"So, tomorrow it is lads. Good luck."

The next day was a special day. The gang were, quite rightly, very nervous. But it dawned bright and warm.

The sun shone and the birds sang. What could possibly go wrong?

Davy was first on the scene. No problems getting the ladder and everything worked like a dream. He whistled happily as he went about his business. Finally he stood back to admire his handiwork. Micky'll be pleased. He looked at his watch. It must all be starting to happen now.

Ron hung around the petrol station. It wasn't very nice by the emergency exit: just dirty old rubbish bins. Still, he had a good view.

After a few moments of looking along the road, he started back and nearly knocked over one of the bins. Party two were coming. Or was it party one? He couldn't remember. OK, anyway, it was all starting to happen. He slipped away round the side of the building.

Davy had managed to get to the house without being seen. It was all quiet. He knew where to go and didn't waste any time. He got a couple of carrier bags and filled them with the stuff he needed and left again.

He'd seen Al doing his bit on his way over here and now he had to catch up as much as he could without being seen.

Micky was also making his way to the rendezvous. He was the most nervous. This had been his idea and he wanted it to go off perfectly.

He and his companion turned off the road and walked through the park gates. It was quiet now and Micky suggested they walk towards the Old Deer Park. It had once been enclosed and its uneven ground, together with roughly planted trees, contrasted sharply to the neat manicured lawns and straight pathways of the rest of the park.

It was starting to get dark now and, as they got closer to the rendezvous, Micky could see Al coming in the opposite direction. Close behind him, Davy was walking quickly, trying to keep the stuff in the two carrier bags quiet. Micky looked over his shoulder and saw Ron catching him up.

He smiled. It was all going to run like clockwork.

The gang all stopped. Al took the arm of his companion, a small old lady. Micky's companion smiled and, with a puzzled look on his face, turned to Micky.

"What's going on son?"

"Yeah, what's this all about?" The woman echoed.

Micky nodded at Davy who had put down the carrier bags. Davy dashed off the path and they heard a click.

All of a sudden they were stood in a pool of light. Fairy lights lit up the trees and formed an accompaniment for the star of the show: a park bench.

"Happy anniversary Mum," Micky said, bending down and picking the woman up in a hug.

She laughed. "Don't be daft, put me down."

He put her down gently and turned to the man. "Happy Anniversary Dad," offering a ground-level hug this time.

Mum and Dad went and sat on the park bench.

"Read the inscription," Ron urged.

*'To Mum & Dad who met at this spot 50 years ago.*
*We're glad they did!*
*From your loving sons: Micky, Ron, Al and Davy'*

It bore today's date.

Davy took out the champagne bottles.

"I thought we were having that at home later," Mum said.

"No, this is better Mum." Al offered her a glass.

"We'll have a toast and then we're gonna give you some time on your own so we'll stay by the park gates and make sure you're not disturbed."

Dad laughed, "I think I may be a bit too old to worry about being disturbed son."

Micky raised his glass and the rest fell silent.

"To Love," he said looking at his parents. "May we all find a love like yours."

The glasses clinked against each other. "To Love" echoed around the park.

# Winning Entry, 2006

Lydia Jones, Derrington, Staffordshire

Losing a Mate

I've made a terrible mistake.

Sitting here on this park bench, so much is obvious.

Damp seeps through the flimsy fabric of my mini skirt; my denim jacket doesn't do much to protect me from early morning mist that slinks between buttons like an unwelcome hand.

I feel conspicuous in last night's party clothes; like anyone who passes will smile in that oh-so-horrible all-knowing way. Not that anyone does pass. Too early.

Plump green cushions of moss nestle in corners of the bench. I pick at them with last night's chipped nail-polished fingers.

From here I can see Shaun's window: the chink where the curtain doesn't quite pull across; the towel discarded on the windowsill. Disorientating to be looking at them from down here, when so recently I was part of the picture they frame. Behind that curtain Shaun is sleeping; white sheets wound around white skin.

It was at the petrol station it happened.

"Just want to give Gertrude a drink before we set off," Shaun said.

"Please do. We don't want the old wreck conking out on us on the way to the party."

"Now, now. You'll hurt her feelings." He turned to

pull down the hose.

Shaun's my best mate at uni. Well, he was. We stabilise each other against the tide of pretentious arrogance that surrounds us. That's the trouble with being the token comprehensive kid. They let you in. But that doesn't mean you fit in.

It was when he was walking back to the car after paying. What was it?

The harsh kiosk light made a halo of his unruly red curls. He dipped his head slightly as he bent to put his wallet in the back pocket of his jeans.

Nothing. It was nothing. Except something flipped over inside.

I watched him walk back to me across the forecourt with that lazy lopsided gait of his, and a tiny nugget of something fizzed into life. It was as if I'd never seen him. I must have looked as gob-smacked as I felt.

"What are you staring at then?"

He opened the door, letting in petrol fumes. Giving me time to recover.

"Don't know. But the label says 'Made in Ireland', so maybe I should check for faults. What do you reckon?"

"You're a cheeky cow, so you are."

He smiled and the fizzing started again.

Shit! Not Shaun.


The party was hardly the usual end of term student bash.

"They hired a church hall for their party? Perlease!"

Shaun quirked an eyebrow. "Wouldn't want to spoil the nice house Daddy paid for, now would we?"

Inside however it was business as usual. Music blared, people hovered around an ever-diminishing drinks table and some brave souls staggered in disjointed attempts at dancing.

I soon lost Shaun to the smoky blackness, but found myself constantly looking out for him. Each fresh glimpse of carrot-topped head, bobbing in conversation, thrown back in laughter, sent the fizzing gremlin inside into overdrive. Get a grip, Faith. Get a grip.

Whenever he saw me looking, his smile was like a soft woollen blanket I wanted to wrap myself inside.

I don't remember how it started. Gatecrashers, someone said. Local kids with a grudge against students. In what seemed like seconds, the hall was a mass of flailing arms, kicking feet. People were screaming. I saw a guy's face covered in blood, heard the dull thud of boot on bone. Panic rose up in an ugly column to my throat. There was no escape. More of them poured through the door; an army of shaved heads and baseball caps.

Suddenly his hand on my arm.

"Faith, this way."

An Irish knight in time of need.

He led me through the kitchen.

"Where the hell...?"

He leant on the silver bar above the green sign. It didn't budge. Inside noise was growing closer. Trouble was spreading.

Shaun swore under his breath. "What good is an emergency exit that doesn't open?"

The second time he threw himself against it the wooden panels beneath buckled. The door gave way. We ran out into the freezing safety of the night-time street.

"How did you know?" I asked, when my breathing slowed enough to make speech possible.

His profile in the streetlight was grim.

"When you're from Belfast, you learn to check for emergency exits first."

So much I don't know about him. So many shadows unexplored. Now I might never get the chance.

We stopped off for a bottle of Jameson's. Lethal stuff. I don't usually drink it.

"What's the matter?"

He was fumbling in a back pocket. I leant against his front door, cursing the non-insulating properties of my denim.

"Come on Shaun. Open the door for God's sake. I'm freezing to death out here."

"I can't find the key."

"What do you mean you can't find the key? Where did you put it?"

"It was in my back pocket. With my wallet. Where it always is."

"You lost your door key out of your pocket? And this is the streetwise Belfast kid I'm supposed to admire?"

"Got you out of trouble, didn't I?" He sounded peeved.

"Yeah, sorry. Thanks, by the way."

I touched his arm. I've done that thousands of times before. But this time... I don't know. The dark, my already alcohol-fuzzed head, the ridiculous fizzing inside. It felt like I was falling towards him. For a second I thought he felt it too.

Instead he slapped his hand hard against the brickwork.

"What the hell do we do now?"

"Wait for Mike and Carl to come back?"

"Mike's at Ally's. Carl's gone home."

"Shit!"

"Exactly."

"Come on."

Suddenly he was heading around the back of the terrace to the little alleyway that runs between this and the houses behind.

"Now where?"

"I've just remembered the landlord keeps a ladder in the shed out back. My room window won't shut properly. If I can get up, I can get in."

He picked the shed lock with ease. Something I probably don't want explained.

So there I was in the early hours of the morning, shivering at the foot of a steel ladder, watching Shaun's trainers slide their way up the silver rungs. He'd drunk too much to be doing this. I'd drunk too much to be holding it steady. My fingers gripped the icy metal with determination and I prayed to whoever was listening that Shaun wouldn't slip.

It must have been the Jameson's that did it. Or the trauma. Or both. We crossed that line that once crossed can never be uncrossed. And now I've lost the best mate I've ever had.

I'm still picking at the moss on the bench, so I don't see him approach. His hair's all messed up from sleep. He's shoved feet into shoes without socks. White skin against black leather.

He sits on the damp bench. I start to speak, but he puts his finger over my lips, then replaces it with his mouth.

"Now for the love of God, woman, will you come back to bed? This park bench is freezing."

Maybe not a mistake, then.

Rebecca Smith, Bingley, West Yorkshire

## The Meaning of Life

I find myself getting impatient travelling to the art exhibition, when Hailey pulls in to the petrol station. Surely this could have been done before she picked me up, I don't even want to go – I'd rather go shoe shopping. Be reasonable, I thought: a couple of glasses of wine the other night and you'd agreed to it.

"The exhibition is about the meaning of life, it's by an up and coming artist, I think it will be fabulous!" gushes Hailey.

It's nice that she can get so enthused about spending a sunny day indoors wandering round in almost silence, but it's not really my thing. I consider suggesting that rather than pondering on the meaning to life, we should just get on with living it.

Finally we arrive; as we make our way through the gallery, I find myself amused as she develops a 'know-it-all strut.'

"I believe it's in the east exhibition room," she calls back to me as we move at a fast pace; she can't wait to get the lesson started. I feel a twinge of resentment: I know she is only explaining things to be kind, but somehow it comes across as a need to feel superior.

My first thought on arrival at the exhibition is there is hardly anything here. This doesn't seem to bother Hailey; she lets out a little squeal of excitement.

"Isn't it marvellous?" she smiles.

I smile back and nod; to be honest I really don't think much of it. For a start it's modern art –

seemingly random items, and no paintings. I always find this sort of thing very difficult to interpret as I'm never sure exactly what I'm supposed to see. But thankfully it should only take a short time to look around. I feel my mood lifting: maybe we'll be out of here before lunch after all.

"Wow! How insightful!" she exclaims.

All I see is a ladder.

"You see how this ladder is leaning against the wall?" – I nod.

"This represents the aspirations of the human race: we strive for success, always wanting more. The fact that you have to look up to the top is a depiction of the way in which people look up to their idols, envying what others have achieved. Even the most successful person has to look upwards to see the top, which suggests that no matter what you have, you still want more; it's human nature never to be completely satisfied."

I see her point, but in all honesty a ladder represents a window cleaner to me – a thought I keep to myself.

The next piece, a park bench, is the only other large item in the room. Hailey is studying it. I stand by her side quietly; what are we supposed to see? It is just a standard bench, nothing exciting about it – could probably do with a lick of paint, but I fail to see anything significant about it. The truth is, if she hadn't stopped to consider its artistic merit I would have sat down, not realising it was part of the exhibit.

"This is very interesting; a bench is associated with resting. This piece represents the need sometimes to stop, and watch the world go by. Life moves at such a pace that often we miss out on the beauty of nature. It reminds us that we should take a closer look at the world around us, and appreciate how good it is to be alive."

I glance round this nearly empty room. What a

strange individual, did he fashion this exhibition from items around his house? It seems a shame they have dedicated a space this size to this particular artist's thoughts on life. There is so much room; it's quite disappointing they haven't let someone else use the other end.

Hailey moves on. I can't see what she is looking at; she is staring at the floor.

"Brilliant!" she whispers.

I do admire her ability to appreciate this kind of art, yet at the same time I do feel it is a little pretentious of the artist to expect the general public to be able to understand his intent without any form of information, not even a small booklet. I would have walked right past this key on the floor without Hailey.

"This is the key to life. Although it is here in the physical form, it is only a representation as no one knows what the meaning of life really is. It's one thing that everyone, regardless of race, education and social status thinks about; it is what we as human beings have in common."

I stand there nodding. I can't help but think it might have dropped out of someone's pocket; there is nothing here to even indicate that it is part of the exhibition.

My thoughts are interrupted. "Do you have any questions?" asks Hailey.

I really don't want to offend her, I know she thinks I'm uncultured – but I really want to know why so much space has been given to three items, so I ask.

"The reason for living is different for each person: for some it's family, for others it's achieving success. The white walls signify that when we are born we are a blank canvas: we make our own picture by every decision and action we take over the course of our lives – it's only at death that the canvas is complete and people can see who we really were."

I stand for a minute, then turn to leave.

"Wait!" calls Hailey, "I want to look at the last piece."

I look around. I can't see anything else, unless the air-conditioning unit is supposed to represent something. I dutifully follow her across the room. We stop, looking at an emergency exit sign. I glance at her unhappy face.

"This is upsetting," she whispers.

"The sign above the door represents those individuals who feel that they cannot cope with life. They feel lost in the world and want to leave before their time is up."

To be honest I think this is genuinely an emergency exit sign and not a representation of suicide, but I stand there as she continues to consider it.

Finally she turns to leave. I am relieved. I'm not a massive fan of art, and this exhibition has been most confusing. Give me a painting of a bowl of fruit any day, at least I know what I'm looking at. I grab a museum leaflet on the way out, in the hope that there will be some information so I can make sense of the exhibition in my own time.

On the car ride home she is buzzing with excitement. I flick through the pamphlet. My eyes scan the page; I stop at the east exhibition room. "Closed – under maintenance."

It seems the 'meaning of life' was in the south wing of the museum.

I fold the leaflet and smile to myself. I guess it proves her point. Everyone sees the meaning of life as something different – she can see it in inanimate objects, whereas I'm bound to find it in a shoe shop this afternoon.

Dave Jobson, Grimsby

Pat's Code

"Got it!" he shouted. "Again, Chemyl! Once more might do it," cried Patrick as he reaffirmed his grip on the makeshift battering ram. Another giant swing and more splintering and cracking left a hole in the wooden fire door a few inches wide. Two more barging swings with the bench they had purloined from the adjacent park a few minutes previously caused the hinges on of the emergency exit door to give way and they could force their way through. "That'll do," he gasped breathlessly. They put the bench down and sat on it for a moment as if to catch their breath. Chemyl wanted to ask what they were doing and found it difficult to believe they were here, but then she knew she had to look after him. He was vulnerable.

"Pat, what exactly am I doing here? What are we doing?" she demanded as he made a show of emptying out his pockets.

"It's written," he replied quietly. He examined the contents in the palm of his hand and poked at a bronze key.

"What's that?" Chemyl enquired.

"That's the key to the front door."

"The front door of what?"

"Of this office," he calmly declared.

"Then why aren't we using it?"

"We can't. It's written."

"What's written? What are we doing here?"

They sprung back into life at the sudden wailing of the alarm going off inside the building.

"Come on!" he cried. "We might not have much time!"

"Pat, no! Not now," Chemyl shouted, but he had already worked his way inside through the breach in the door and down the corridor of the small building. "Aaarrgghh! Pat! Wait!" She reluctantly ran inside after him. Whatever it was they were doing, they would have to do it quickly now. "Where are you, Pat?" she shouted as she felt her way uncertainly through the darkness of the unlit, windowless corridor that had swallowed him up.

"Wait a minute," he replied from somewhere in front of her. Her eyes were immediately assaulted by the explosion of light as the corridor bulbs in front of and behind her struck into dazzling life.

"What are we doing here anyway?" she begged him. "Can't you tell me? Pat? Where are you?"

As her eyes adjusted to the light, she saw a door ajar before her and she walked towards it, uncertainly. She pushed it open and browsed the dilapidated interior of the petrol station shop, seeing the dented, dust-covered cans of oil, tattered maps, and broken indicator bulbs. Business wasn't so good. She remembered the rumour she had heard that the owner and his brother both had expensive operations to pay for, which meant they couldn't reinvest in the garage.

Her attention was abruptly hijacked by the sounds above her head as a heavy groaning and creaking sound was accompanied by the ceiling collapsing around her. She dived out of the way. "Oh my God. What's going on," she muttered to herself. "Pat," she cried. "The police are outside. What are you looking for?"

She worked her way forward through the debris of the roof plaster and rotten beams, to where she could see him through the gaping hole in the ceiling as he stepped from beam to beam in the attic of the building.

The voice on the loudhailer came across loud and muffled from outside as the nervous young police officer fumbled with the controls and didn't hold the thing close enough to his mouth. They couldn't discern his words but the sentiment wasn't overlooked.

Pat took another false step and this time fell through the floor, landing awkwardly in the middle of the room, bringing more plaster and dust down.

"Are you all right?" asked Chemyl as she helped him to his feet. "The police are outside, and I think I saw Mr Bannister, the owner of the petrol station."

"It's OK, Chemyl." He pulled the folded letter out of his pocket and handed it to Chemyl. She unfolded it and scrutinised it.

"I don't understand this. It's just a letter from Bannister, telling you about his visits to the bank and accountants."

"Don't you see there at the bottom? Can't you see the P.S.? Isn't the anagram obvious?"

Her gaze followed his finger. "Where? So what? Anagram?" She was bewildered. She read the line to herself in the vague hope it may illuminate something within her.

*PS nil loan. This bank unsympathetic. Miracle awaited*

Pat looked amazed that he wasn't making himself understood. He snatched at the letter. "The P.S. stands for Pat Smith – me. It took me a while to work out the rest."

"You think it's an anagram? Of what? What does it say, Pat?"

"It really says,
'*PS Mona Lisa up in attic. Break in and steal with*

*Chemyl.'*

That's why I brought you. Do you see?"

A disbelieving Chemyl scrutinised Pat's face. She gently took the letter from him and examined the sentence. "Pat, that's just a coincidence. Nobody was telling you to break into here and steal the Mona Lisa. This is a petrol station. Have you been reading Dan Brown again? You heard what the therapist told you. You have to leave them alone, Pat. Do you understand?"

"I know but I thought it was an anagram. I really thought he was telling me where the Mona Lisa was. Have I been awfully silly?"

"I think so, Pat," said Chemyl gently ruffling Pat's hair. "You'll have to go with the police now. They'll take you to the station and ask you some questions but I'll come and see you later and make everything all right. OK?"

"OK."

She walked out ahead of Pat so she could get to the police officer first. Bannister was also standing there, grinning, as she apologised for her friend's behaviour and explained about his condition.

"Thanks, Chemyl," said Pat as the policeman started to lead him away. "I'll see you later."

"Officer!" declared Chemyl. "Just before you leave, you might want to take Bannister with you."

The young officer looked unnerved. "I do? Why?"

"Because he is committing the crime of attempting to defraud an insurance company to help his obviously ailing business and you have lots of questions for him."

"I do?" the officer spluttered.

"Yes, because the line

*'PS nil loan. This bank unsympathetic. Miracle awaited'*

is indeed an anagram, isn't it, Bannister." His grin

had gone and he was squirming as she observed him. "If you examine it officer, you will find that it reads:

*'Will bait Pat Smith kid. Insurances can pay to heal men.'*

You set Pat Smith up to damage your garage for the insurance, hoping he would destroy it, didn't you? You've been siphoning money out of this business to pay for your medical costs." She turned to the policeman. "Take him away officer. I'll clean up here."

Waiting until everyone had gone, she used the ladder leaning up against the sidewall to climb up into the attic through the gaping hole, finding the Mona Lisa she knew to be there. She already had her buyer. And Brazil awaited.

It had gone very well.

Lucy Brown, Wakefield

Weddings and Wisdom

"Have you got everything?" Liz queried, leaning against the wall as Sarah fumbled in her handbag for her house key.

"Got it," she muttered triumphantly as she dug it out. "I think so." For a moment Sarah surveyed the door with her hand still attached. "Something's wrong."

"It's a door, Sar."

"Not that; look!" She proffered the hand. "My engagement ring! Where is it?"

"Oh... Check back inside."

Following the command, Sarah disappeared. For nearly twenty minutes Liz heard various curses coming from the other side of the threshold but made no effort to help. Eventually, Sarah re-emerged, locking the door. "It's not there. What's Tim going to say?"

"Y'know, I doubt he'll notice."

"Of course he'll notice! He bought it!"

On that logic, Liz replied quietly, "Maybe it's a sign."

Either Sarah was pretending she hadn't heard or she actually hadn't. "Maybe I left it at work, I remember having it there. And I have to take it off when the carwash plays up so—"

"You wanna check?"

"We've got time, haven't we?"

"Sure. Let's go."

Less than fifteen minutes later, Liz pulled onto the forecourt of the petrol station. Before her foot fully hit the brake Sarah was out and away, lifting up her skirts as she skipped over puddles. Liz parked then followed her into the service station.

Matthew Bowyer stood behind the till reading a woman's magazine and looking thoroughly bored. The tiny shop was fully stocked, almost fit to bursting with mints, cigarettes and dateless accessories – it was as ill-used as ever then. Squeezing past the water bottles Liz was on Sarah's heels as she reached the counter. Behind Matthew the glass door showed the height of the sun, Liz calculating they still had enough time: early preparation had its merits after all.

"Matt!" Sarah screeched after he failed to be roused by their entrance.

He looked up, somewhat surprised. "Didn't you have the day off?" After a moment he shrugged. "My mistake. All right, float's in the till, Mr Rawlins is due in anytime for—"

"Matt," interrupted Sarah. "I'm not working today."

"You're not?"

"OK," she said, regulating her breathing. "What am I wearing?"

"A white dress," he answered. "What?"

Liz turned to hide the smirk on her face.

"You know what, forget it!" Sarah burst out. "Let me past, I've lost something."

"Like what?"

"Oh, move! Lizzie, help me."

Complying, she let Matthew pass her before joining the bride-to-be at the other side of the counter. After a fruitless search of the top the pair ended up on all fours, Liz conscious of the dirt they were scrabbling in.

Dimly, she registered the main door opening and shutting then lifted her ears up as a voice yelled, "This is a robbery!"

Glancing at Sarah, she muttered, "Oh, great."

Her friend was obviously horrified. Her eyes widened and her fingernails scratched at the tile. Recognising the beginning of a panic attack Liz looked desperately around. The counter was high enough to shield them both: until, of course, Mr Robber got to the till. The panic button installed in every station was situated just under the wooden top at the far side of Sarah and, since the chances of her regaining her senses to reach it were limited, it was a no-go. After all, if she tried to lean across Sarah either the blonde would collapse or her fingers would alert Mr Robber. Either way they were target practice.

Looking to the right her eyes latched onto the door and the 'emergency exit' sign above it. Sarah followed her gaze; she knew what was needed so an instant later Liz made a decision, pushing the door open slightly and crawling onto the porch it led to. Voices from inside indicated that Matthew was resisting so Liz held out a hand. A moment later they were safely outside.

"Come on," said Liz quickly. "I'll call the police on the way."

A few streets away there was a park and that was where the duo collapsed onto a bench, Liz feeling this was another omen but not daring to say so.

After a minute of silence Sarah shook her left leg. "I knew I shouldn't have run in these."

Boots... All right.

"Why, what's up?"

"I think a button slipped inside or something. Hang on," she added, tugging the lace and removing the boot. She tipped it upside down and onto the gravel fell a small circular object – not a button. "Oops."

"That's not what I think it is?"

"It might be." Sarah took the ring, sliding it on her finger. "I remember now. I put it there for safe-keeping."

Despite her anger at the whole almost-getting-taken-hostage thing, Liz had to laugh. "Yeah, I think that worked!"

Sarah joined in. "I was nervous about losing it on the day."

"So you put it in your shoe?"

"You make it sound irrational."

"Oh, do I?" Liz pulled her phone from her bag to check the time. "It's quarter to."

Sarah sobered up. "We've got fifteen minutes!"

"We'll make it."

Grabbing her by the hand, Liz whizzed them through the park, again thanking her parents she'd been brought up in an area rife with crime and full of shortcuts. Soon they were outside the civic office, right in front of a collection of 'out of order' signs which were taped to each doorway.

Sarah sank. "No!"

"You have to be kidding me." Nabbing a nearby official, Liz queried, "How can a building be out of order?"

The woman smiled apologetically. "The automatic doors have malfunctioned and the emergency exits are padlocked."

"Oh, that's safe!"

"Yes, well... I'm sorry, do you have a reservation?"

Liz snorted. "We did."

"All reservations still stand," the woman objected silkily. "All we require is... flexibility."

"What do you mean?" asked Liz suspiciously.

"We respectfully ask that anybody wishing to keep an appointment today should climb through the upper window using this ladder."

Raising her eyes upwards, Liz swallowed and inwardly questioned why civic buildings were huge. Obviously, no one anticipated events like this. "You want us to climb up there?"

"Call it a labour of love."

"I can do it," said Sarah instantly. "And he'll be waiting."

"Oh, Sar!" Liz burst out incredulously. "Can't you rearrange it?"

"It's the final test!"

"Yeah, it just might be!"

"Lizzie... Please?"

The pitiful eyes did it. Sighing, Liz took hold of the ladder, wincing as, at every rung, she trod on her already blackened bridesmaid gown. At the top there was a woman to hoist her in and Liz asked, "Can you tell Timothy Nunn his bride's here?"

"Of course."

Once the woman had disappeared Liz looked through the window. Sarah was climbing like a demented monkey, not minding the state her dress was getting into. When she was close enough, Liz held out a hand to help her in. "You got rid of your vertigo then?"

Sarah was grinning like an imbecile. "I feel so alive! Like I've really had to work for it! Now I feel worthy."

Liz kept her tongue in check on that one as the woman returned. "Did you find him?"

She looked very uncomfortable. "I'm sorry. Mr Nunn cancelled half an hour ago."

Peter Morris, Skelmersdale

## Community Service

"Well your honour, what actually happened was that I had been working hard. I mean, I know me forms say that I'm unemployed, but I'm sort of not, if ye know what I mean. There was this old woman who lived next door to me, well, a couple of doors away in the next street, and she couldn't walk and she was blind and stuff. So one day I saw her having trouble getting out of her house in her wheelchair, so I helped her get out and then pushed her down the shops and then took her home. I mean, she offered to give me some money but I didn't take any cause I was signing on.

"Anyway, she asked me to help her do some more stuff a couple of days later and then she asked me to help a friend of hers. I mean I took her to the bingo and the cinema and shopping and stuff and I never took nothing for it. I was really enjoying it and thought I might be able to use it to get a job like. I mean I had been inside once and it's hard to get a job after that especially if you haven't got any training or stuff. So, I thought that as long as I wasn't getting paid it was all right and that after a while I might be able to get a real job helping people, like a social worker or something.

"So anyway, I ended up working six or seven days every week. I mean I didn't plan it. It just sort of happened. One of the people I helped said that they had a house down here at the seaside and that if I ever wanted to get away I could use their house for a couple of days. They said they were selling it, so it didn't matter about when I went down, as there was never no one there. She wasn't one of me regulars, she was a friend of one of them and she was just passing through so I never really got to know her name or nothing, she just wrote down the address on a piece of paper and told me that the key was under the flower pot beside the door.

"Well, your honour, I came down here by train. I walked all the way from the station, cause I was skint, and when I got to the shore front I just walked around enjoying the sound of the waves and stuff. I found the row of houses where this woman had lived and I counted along till I got to number thirty-four, that's where she said she lived. The sun was shining so that the front of the houses was dark but the other side of the road, the sea side, was dead bright so I stayed on that side. Right opposite the house was a park bench. It had a plaque on it and I turned it round so I would get some sun on me face and I sat down. I must have been really tired cause I fell asleep and as those witnesses said, I was there for some time your honour, I wasn't sizing up the place like they all thought; I was asleep.

"I woke up about teatime and I felt a bit cold. So I went over to the house. I checked it was number thirty-four cause there was no flowerpot outside the front door, so I couldn't find the key. I didn't really know what to do your honour. It was too late to get a train back and I had no money for bed and breakfast nor nothing, so I looked through the windows just like the witnesses said they saw me doing. I went round the back in case there was a key under a flower pot there and saw that someone had broke in to the house using a ladder up to the second floor and then come out the back door.

"I had a quick look round and couldn't find no tools or nothing to fix the door. I had seen a petrol station on me way down, so I decided to walk to it and get a padlock or something to lock the door and get meself something hot to eat while I was at it. It was pretty dark by now so I pulled the door over and made my way up to the petrol station. It was one of them twenty-four hour jobs but the main door hadn't been locked yet. It was a pretty big place your honour, I mean, it sold everything, so I went in and was really pleased to see that they sold tools. They didn't have any chains or locks or stuff like that so I got one of them wire baskets and took a small crowbar cause I knew that I should be able to jam the door closed and probably fix it. I took a big screwdriver and pliers and I got some sandwiches and some drink, then I went to the toilet your honour.

"When I came out I was in a bit of a dream cause the toilet is right next door to the counter and I think the bright lights blinded me. I needed some ciggies so I wasn't thinking your honour and as you can see from the video I just walked over and took a couple of packets and dropped them in me basket. That was when I realised that the garage fella was over at the main doors locking them. He started yelling at me and I thought he had a gun so the only thing I could do was run away out through the emergency door. I wasn't thinking and I panicked which is probably how the cash got into me pocket, but all I was thinking about was that the fella was going to kill me and as you can see on the video he does chase me and scream at me. I ran for me life and never stopped till I got back to the house. I got in and I didn't switch any lights on cause I didn't know if he had followed me all the way back.

"I spent the night on the settee your honour, just in case anyone broke in and the next morning I made sure that no one could get in through the back door by jamming the dining table up against it. Then your honour I noticed that the house was still full of ornaments and stuff so I had a look round and knowing that the old woman was a bit short of memory I packed two suitcases with bits and pieces which I thought she would like. I was gonna call in the petrol station, apologise for what had happened and give them their stuff back, before getting the train home your honour and it was just as I was coming out of the front door that the police got me. And that's the truth your honour."

Brian Lockett, London

## An Urban Adventure

"Is this some kind of joke? If it is, then I think you'd better explain."

Gerald Thurston, FRPS, threw the five photographs down on the table and glared at the young man who had just handed them to him. He prided himself on his professionalism and expected high standards from others in the photographic world in which he moved.

"No joke, Mr Thurston. These are my entries for the club's photographic competition this year. And you are the independent judge who has been taken on to make the choice."

"The rules, young man, are that five photographs on a single theme must be submitted. You have produced no more than – well, let's be kind and call them snaps, of everyday objects that can be found almost anywhere. They are of no great merit, technical or artistic. There is nothing in the way of composition, delicate use of light and shade or any of the usual things we judges look for. In addition there is no theme whatsoever."

"Well, let's look at it this way, Mr Thurston. Photograph number 1 is the key to the flat of a certain married woman. The car – photograph number 2 – if you look at it a little more closely, I think you will find is yours at a petrol filling station just round the corner from that flat. According to the data in my camera it was taken at 10 o'clock yesterday morning. The emergency exit sign, you will recall seeing as you left the flat rather hurriedly when the lady's husband's car unexpectedly arrived in the car park. Unfortunately, the emergency exit was locked, which brings me to photograph number 4 – the ladder. It had, happily for you, been left behind leaning against the wall by a builder and provided you with an essential means of escape. That was when the key fell out of your pocket."

Gerald Thurston was looking pale.

"And the park bench?" he whispered.

"Ah, yes," said the young man. "The park bench. Well, that just makes up the number and happened to be in the area when I was photographing. But I don't think that really matters, do you?"

"And the theme?" said Thurston hoarsely.

"What about 'An Urban Adventure'? Or you can think up your own title, if you like. I'm not fussy. The important thing is that I have won the £1,000 first prize. Can we agree on that? I'll see you on judging day then."

And the young man left quickly, leaving a rather pompous professional staring into space.

Annette Reader, Huntingdon

## A Place Not Found on the Internet

The Rusk biscuit begs the question; where did it go? I mean, it must've gone somewhere. Another time, maybe? Another world? Another dimension?

I don't know. Maybe I never will. Wherever it went, I can't find it on the internet.

One person does know, but I can't ask her. Instead, my sub-conscious whispers fevered solutions; places which haunt my dreams. Barren deserts which dehydrate living creatures, leaving desiccated, empty husks. Storm-swept wastelands occupied by creatures whose howls merge with the wind causing a sound so primal it turns a person's guts inside out. Black voids crushing light and sound and air into dense little pockets of nothing. Each time it's different and each time I wake up gasping and terrified, chanting my mantra that has become a prayer 'I didn't mean to do it, I didn't mean to do it.'

What I do know is the Rusk answers one question; it survived the journey.

It first happened when I was a baby, not that anyone knew then what I was capable of. We were in a petrol station. Mum had just filled up our old blue car and then she went inside to pay, taking me with her. I'd been grizzling for days; she was exhausted and desperate for me to settle but once inside I fell silent. She noticed I'd become fascinated by the Emergency Exit sign. At first she was happy I was occupied but then my expression disturbed her, something about the intensity of my gaze. "He looked like a sinner who'd just found God," she later told my father. To distract me she gave me her house key to play with.

That was the last time it was seen.

It was the first thing I sent. Since then my parents became used to misplacing stuff. It was one of those things – until my mother disappeared. The Police and our neighbours suspected my father, but by then we both knew better. I've tried to reassure him that it won't happen again, but he doesn't believe me. Even now I catch him staring at me like a fawn trapped in a lift with a sleeping bear.

Over the years I've got used to my gift, come to control it, even. In my lifetime I have sent thousands of objects. Many, like the house key, I've not realised I've sent. The majority I've forgotten. Some things though, were precious. It wasn't until they were gone that I realised how much I needed them. These should never have been sent but at first I found it hard to control my gift especially when I was angry or tired or hungry... well, you try not to think of a pink elephant when a blush-coloured pachyderm is all you can think of.

It's easy to send stuff. It's once they've gone the problems begin. I mean, how am I supposed to feel about something which just isn't *there* anymore. If it was broken or dead or lost you'd mourn its passing. But this? My dad has it cracked. He sits by the door waiting for her to return. I wish it was that simple.

I don't bother sending stuff these days – I mean, what's the point? It doesn't matter what I send or how often, I can't get anything back. Not that I haven't tried. I've pictured Entrance signs, doors, vehicles... well; it would take forever to list everything I've tried. Nothing worked.

Until now.

It was the tramp who showed me. He was sat on the bench in the park, hunched up against one of the arms. The paint had peeled revealing grey wooden slats as if the alcohol fumes he was emitting had stripped it off.

"Fushing, sushing manks!" he cried out as I approached, leaping up off the bench and accosting me, hugging his bottle as though it were a delicate newborn.

I'd had a really bad day and I wanted to get home. I know; it's a lousy excuse, but before I knew it, I'd visualised the Emergency Exit sign and he was gone, leaving a slight whiff of ozone behind him.

Glancing around the park, wondering if anyone else witnessed my guilty secret, a glint from behind the trees caught my attention. A ladder. It had been dumped by fly-tippers, but for some reason it caught my eye. Adrenaline flooded through my veins making my mouth dry and my heart pump hard, I felt like I had discovered gravity. So simple, why hadn't I thought of it before? And then I realised, maybe I just wasn't meant to.

I started to run home. As I did an argument raged inside my head; it wouldn't work – I had tried and failed so many times; it would work – I had been too literal before. What else was a ladder but something to get from one level to another?

That night I concentrated on the ladder; the dirt ingrained in the silver ridges of the rungs, the black rubber feet, everything I could remember.

I don't know what I expected to see when I opened my eyes, but I was sure something would come back
Nothing did.

I then concentrated on all the things I remember sending. The broken plastic duck I sent in frustration because it no longer quacked. Some maths homework I couldn't complete because it was too difficult. A mate's lunch I sent as a practical joke when I was ten. My mother. I tried to conjure up the sound of her voice trying to soothe my temper tantrum just before she vanished from existence. I imagined each of them climbing the ladder.

Still nothing came back. I went to bed with disappointment so acute it made my head hurt. It was over. I didn't know what else to try.

The next morning I endured an agony I never knew existed. It felt as though my bones were being ground into dust. I didn't leave my bed for four days.

When the pain had finally abated enough for me to leave my room, the first thing I saw was a gold house key.

That was over a week ago. Since then I've had the energy to retrieve only two more things. I think they're coming back in the order in which I sent them.

The Rusk arrived back this morning; it waylaid my biggest fear. That's the thing about the key, although it came back perfect: it's metal. If I sent it to another solar system how would I recognise space dust or pock marks made by alien meteorites? A big gold house key doesn't appreciate time. It doesn't need to eat or breathe for twenty years. Or rot. Rusk biscuits do. But this one came back as perfect as the day I sent it. It wasn't stale or anything. Just in case, I ate it. It was delicious.

It will take time to get everything back. Briefly I wonder if she'll sound the same. Hell, will she *be* the same. A Rusk is not a sentient being. It has no mind to send to another dimension. What about *her* mind, where did I send that?

I don't know. Hopefully it won't be long before I find out.

Catriona Child, Edinburgh

## I Want to Break Free

Susie's parents were sitting on the bench. They'd been there for ages now, even though her dad had promised he'd come and play Ring-a-ring-a-rosies in ten minutes.

"Not now," her mum had said; "mummy needs tae tell daddy somethin' important."

"Whit?" Susie had asked.

"It's just for grown ups," her mother had answered.

"Ah'll play wi' ye soon," her dad had said. "Ten minutes, OK?"

"OK," Susie had replied, "will ye play ring-a-ring-a-rosies?"

"Aye."

"Ye promise?"

"Ah promise."

That had been well over ten minutes ago now, it must have been at least twenty; maybe more. Susie had got bored, and had started playing the spinning game by herself. It was when you twirled round and round with your arms out, then fell over onto the ground all dizzy. It made the park spin, as if the whole world was moving really fast. The trees and flowers became all blurry, and you couldn't see them very well; like the time she'd put on her granny's glasses and tried to watch TV. Her granny had given her a row; told her to take them off or she'd get a sore head.

Susie looked at her parents; they were sitting at opposite ends of the bench. Her dad had his head in his hands; her mum tried to put her arm round him but he pushed it away. Susie liked her mum's cuddles; she felt soft, and smelt of perfume. Her dad's cuddles were different, but still good. They were stronger, and she always got her face scratched by his bristles. She wondered why he didn't want to cuddle her mum.

"Da' whit's wrong?"

"Nothin' sweetie, don't worry."

"How come ye didnae want cuddled then?"

"Ah a'ways want cuddled." He reached down and picked Susie up. He pulled her close, tighter than normal; squeezing her until she had to tell him she couldn't breathe anymore.

"Sorry pet," he released his grip, "ah didnae mean it."

His voice sounded funny, like he needed to wipe his nose.

"Right, time tae go," said her mum.

"But we havnie played ring-a-ring-a-rosies yet. Da' ye promised."

"Promises are no a'ways enough, are they?" Her dad replied.

"That's no fair Iain."

"Whit's no fair mummy?"

"Shh Susie!"

"Dinnae take it out on her Louise, she's no done anythin'."

"Look we're goin' home, there's things ah need tae dae."

"Have ye no done enough a'ready?"

Her mum didn't say anything, just looked at the ground; like she'd spilt juice on the good carpet or something.

"Whit's mummy done?"

"Nothin' pet," her dad replied, "let's go tae the car. Ah'll buy ye a sweetie at the garage on the way home."

*

Susie's dad was filling the car with petrol; the smell made her head feel funny, and her nose itch, like she was going to sneeze.

"Ah need tae pee mummy," she said.

"Don't say pee, it's dirty. Say wee-wee."

"Ah need a wee-wee."

"Cin ye no wait till we get home?"

"No, ah'm desperate."

Her mum sighed, getting out of the car.

"Right wait here, ah need tae go an' ask the man fur the key."

"Where are ye goin'?" Susie heard her dad ask.

"Yer daughter needs a piss OK? Do ah have tae report everythin' ah dae?"

"Well, who knows what ye could be up tae?"

Her mum hissed something at Susie's dad, and made a hand signal as she walked off; it was like putting the thumbs up but she used her finger instead. Even though her mum had tried to whisper, Susie still managed to hear what she'd said. She'd never heard her mum use such a bad word before. She must be really angry at her dad. She wondered what he'd done; it must have been something extra bad. Even when Susie had drawn all over the living room wall, her mum had only used the 'bloody' word.

"Come on." Susie's mum opened the car door, motioning for Susie to get out. Susie followed her as she led the way to the toilet. Her mum was walking really fast, and Susie had to run to keep up.

"Right, there ye go." Her mum unlocked the door. "Shall ah come in?"

"No, ah cin go masell, gi' me the key."

"Mummy'll keep the key."

"But ah wantae hold it."

"It's best—"

"...please mummy."

"Well... aw'right, but don't lock the door."

"Ah won't."

The key was heavy, but warm from being in her mum's hand; like money when you held it for too long. Susie went into the toilet, and closed the door behind her. It didn't shut properly, so she put the key in the lock and turned it.

"Did ye just lock that door?" Susie heard her mum's muffled voice.

"No mummy... ah promise."

Susie's voice echoed off the grey, concrete walls; like it did in her granddad's shed. It was dark with the door closed; the only light there shone through a tiny window near the ceiling, which had cobwebs on it. She wished she had a ladder so she could climb up and look out; she could wave to her dad as he filled the car.

The toilet smelt funny; it made her think of the dirty washing basket. Susie had climbed in there to hide the day she'd drawn on the wall. She had hidden for ages; so long that she'd fallen asleep in it, and when her mum had found her she'd said that she was so glad to see her she didn't care about the wall anymore. Maybe she should tell her dad to hide there when they got back home.

"Ah dinnae need anymore," she said, going to unlock the door. The key was stiff, and wouldn't budge. She used both hands, clasping them round the key, and pulling at it until it hurt, the metal digging into her skin, leaving a white mark.

"Mummy," she called through the door; there was no answer.

"Mummy, ah'm locked in."

"MUMMY... MUMMY!" Susie began to scream repeatedly; still nobody answered.

Susie's heart was beating so fast, she could feel it inside her chest. She turned, hoping that if she looked at the other end of the room she might find another way out; like the 'mergency exit her gran had taken her through, that day the fire alarm went off in Asda. As she moved, she caught sight of her shadowy reflection in the mirror above the sink. Susie jumped, thinking it was a ghost, before realising it was her own face peering back from the dusty glass. She ran towards the door, banging her body against it, as her hands fumbled with the key. She was crying now, and could hardly see what she was doing through the tears.

"MUMMY... HELP ME... PLEASE!"

There was a loud click, and the door suddenly opened. Susie fell forwards into the daylight, bashing her hip against the door, and landing on her knees on the concrete. Her eyes were all funny; yellow shapes floated in front of them, as if she'd been staring straight at the sun. Her knees were stinging, and blood ran down her leg; she got to her feet looking for her mum and dad.

Her dad was sitting on the front of the car; he had his head in his hands again. He looked up when he saw her, and ran towards her.

"Susie, sweetheart, ma God, whit happened?"

"Mummy... left... me," Susie managed to say through the sobs. There was a lump in her throat, like she'd swallowed a big sweetie without chewing it.

"Me too," her dad replied.

Stephen Lake, Leeds

## The Promise

The old man sitting on the park bench scratched his beard and sighed as he looked down at the busy petrol station lit up in the darkness below. As a child he remembered the panoramic view in front of him being empty fields, dykes and woods. Now it was spoilt with concrete and glowing neon lighting.

He could feel his legs getting cold and stamped his feet to warm them up. What was keeping him? He pulled a sleeve of his jacket back and glanced at his watch. It was ten minutes before midnight, Suddenly a car pulled up behind him and he heard the door close with a thunk as someone approached and sat down on the park bench beside him.

"You've cut it a bit fine Paul," said the old man turning to look at his grandson.

"Don't worry granddad," said Paul fiddling with the car keys in his hand. "There's plenty of time yet."

They sat together in silence watching the endless stream of cars entering the petrol station. The old man was amazed that people were still awake at this time of night, but Paul seemed indifferent to it.

"Are you sure you want to do this?" Paul asked, breaking the silence. "You've thought of the consequences when it hits the fan?"

The old man nodded. "I'm sure."

Paul looked into his granddad's eyes for a few seconds, nodded, and passed him the keys to his car. "You be careful with her granddad. She's a fast car, not like in your day."

Granddad looked over his shoulder to stare at the

sleek polished red car sat waiting behind them and then at Paul's sinewy, young body. He knew he shouldn't be involving Paul in this, but he had no option. There was no way he could climb the ladder. As if he was reading his thoughts Paul slapped him on the arm. "Stop worrying granddad, I'll get her quicker than you can dance the tango."

"Shall we do it then," said granddad, standing up and stretching his aching back. "Now you know what to do, you know which door it is?"

"Yeh, Yeh, I know. It's the third door on the right, before the glass door that has the emergency exit sign above it."

"And don't forget it's the third level – the ladder can't reach that far."

"Relax granddad," said Paul over his shoulder as he walked slowly towards the apartment block, flexing his muscles as he did so. He noted the alarm box on the wall and the security lights on each corner of the building as he lifted the ladder from its hiding place and propped it against the wall. It easily reached the second floor windows. Swiftly climbing the ladder Paul pushed at the landing window. It had been left unlocked for them and it silently opened onto a carpeted corridor. It was quiet and empty; hopefully everyone was fast asleep. Stepping over the window ledge Paul spotted the stairs to the next landing. He glanced at his watch. A couple of minutes to go before midnight; he was on time.

It wasn't long before he was standing outside the third door on the right. There was not a sound as he quickly read the brass nameplate on the wooden door. "Hilary Swank" – yep, this is the one. Gently he pushed the door open...

The old man inserted the key in the ignition and switched on, ready for a quick getaway. The engine purred into life and he noted with a little bit of irritation that the tank was only quarter full. He had given Paul some money to fill her up. Now he would have to visit the petrol station before starting the long journey. He wound his window down and watched the ladder leaning against the wall. Why did this retirement home have all this security equipment around it? It reminded him of a prison.

The car was beginning to warm up nicely when he suddenly heard a shoe scraping on a wall. He looked up and saw Paul climbing over the window ledge with a body draped over his shoulder. Good, he'd got her – and he watched anxiously as his grandson came confidently down the ladder. He wished that he could have been the one to do it, but at his age and with the state of his knees, he knew he wouldn't have been able to.

Reaching the ground Paul carried the body over to the car and on arriving at the passenger door he gently helped the body over his shoulder to stand.

"Yippee!" exclaimed Hilary, punching the air with her fist.

"Shh!" said Paul putting a finger to his lips. "You'll wake them up."

Hilary grinned. "Oops, sorry," she said and then frowned. "My bag, young man, you've forgotten my bag!"

Paul laughed. "I'm going, I'm going, keep your hair on," and ran back to the ladder, climbed to the top once more and reached over the window ledge. Pulling a small canvas bag over it, he slid down the ladder and raced back to the car.

Hilary had jumped into the passenger seat and was hugging the old man. "Isn't this exciting George!" she exclaimed, kissing him on the cheek, her eyes sparkling.

George smiled. "I'm sorry I couldn't climb the ladder

Hilary. I'm a little bit too old for that sort of thing."

Hilary slapped his arm playfully. "Don't be silly, you old fool. It was a lovely idea getting your grandson to carry me down the ladder. You can't elope without going down a ladder first, can you, its tradition!"

George laughed. "Your son will be furious when he finds out, you know that?"

Hilary snorted. "Stuff him," she replied. "It's my life and I can do whatever I please!"

Paul leant into the car and grinned at the two old people acting like two school children. "Remember you two. I want the car back for work Monday morning – oh and I'm sorry," he said reaching into his back pocket and pulling out a twenty pound note. "I forgot to get some petrol granddad."

Hilary took the money. "Don't worry young man, and thank you for helping us. You were brilliant!"

Paul withdrew his head and slapped the roof. "Get off with you and watch your speed."

The old couple smiled at each other. "To Gretna Green," said Hilary laying her head on George's shoulder and squeezing his arm.

"To Gretna Green," replied George as he engaged first gear and slowly drove away.

Babette Gallard, St Aubin Fosse Louvain, France

Deceitful Appearance

Appearances can be deceiving.

What can you see? A man? Late thirties perhaps? Filling his car with petrol just like millions of other people do everyday?

That's right. It's a common scene; nothing special, nothing out of the ordinary, except for what you can't see. My hand, a gory mess hidden in my right pocket, three fingers broken when Her Majesty's morons decided to change the meaning of the words Emergency and Exit, which in my case meant a door slammed in my face.

The idiots are still searching the building, but Josh the Janitor, so new that even his employers don't know him, is long gone. In fact he's on a garage forecourt, doing what anyone else does when they need some petrol.

Yes, I know all the tricks. I've been in the game a long time, perhaps too long, which is why I'm talking to you now, spilling the beans as they say, like the magician who lets his public see the myth behind the magic.

Myth number one: I'm not a janitor, or a window cleaner or any of those other aliases I use.

Myth number two: I'm not two bricks short of a wall, as I need some people to think. No way. I'm a master of my art, available to the highest bidder, which has on occasion included Her Majesty's government, but when you're as good as I am the bids come high and from places people like you probably haven't even heard of.

So what do I do?

I protect secrets that have a price on their head.

How do I do it?

By putting micro-devices, usually eyes and ears, into places no one thinks about or gives a second glance. Let me give you an example.

Today's spy, the techno Kim Philby of the 21$^{st}$ Century, is accessing Top Secret files and downloading them for his own use. Easy, as long as no one can look over his shoulder – except that a superior has become suspicious and called me in.

"Check him out will you? See what he's up to. You know what I mean."

One phone call, one bank transfer and Bob the Builder is on the case.

*Bang, bang, tap, tap.* A trolley full of tools, but no work done, at least not in the building line.

I've seen all I need. Each office door is locked with a personal security code, meaning our man thinks he's safe from unexpected intruders. He is, but no one has bothered to remove the keys still sitting like faithful servants in their old keyholes and waiting to prove that nothing is ever quite what it seems.

I spy with my little eye... a micro camera on a key tip.

Close the door my friend, if it makes you feel safer, but I can still watch you from my flat in Hampstead.

Sometimes the job requires a little more than just seeing and hearing – not my kind of thing really, but I'll do it if the rewards are high enough. I've got the skill after all.

The message comes through: "She's a pain in the arse, takes too many risks and speaks to people I don't like. You know what to do, but make it clean."

Pretty girl, silly girl. I'm tapping into her phone so I know she meets her lover every midday on the same park bench.

Five to twelve a dosser parks his stinking bum there, leaves something sticky behind and then trots on his doleful way.

A sad old man, though not half as sad as she will be when the poison seeps into her summer-bare skin. Who would think that something as simple as a park bench could be so damaging to her health. She's dead before lover boy arrives. Clean.

Then there's the listening. My last job, before I started speaking to you, was on the third floor of a block of council flats, harmless enough on the face of it, but surrounded by goons with guns if you knew where to look.

Eavesdropping can be messy if you make a mistake, but it's easy when you know how and no one challenges me on this particular day, because I'm cleaning windows on a building opposite.

*Wish, wash.* Click in the device that is so focused and powerful it could pick up a fart on the moon. So small you'd think it was just a screw in the ladder. Well, in a way that's what it is, because the blokes opposite are about to be screwed. Someone should have told them never to go on first impressions.

All in a day's work, just another job, and I'm not paying much attention until I listen in to what's being said and get my first reminder that I should practise what I preach.

Well, what do you know? The men inside are servants of Her Majesty and they want to talk to me about some of my clients, but they're not planning to ask nicely. The contact who passed this job on was anonymous, but still good enough to tip me the wink. Maybe he's repaying a favour I did him, but now I'm on my own. No third parties.

Suddenly I'm feeling very lonely, but I never let emotions cloud my judgement. As cold as ice and as clear as crystal, I watch my step, wash my windows and record every word they say. Then I make a tape and send it with a note to the Chief Constable who is behind it all.

*Didn't your mother ever tell you that walls have ears?*

I'm laughing when I do it and still laughing a few days later, but today it's not funny anymore, because I've just walked into an ambush and only got out by the skin of my fingers. There are probably some bits of it still hanging on the door.

I must be losing my touch, but I'm not letting Her Majesty and the boys have the last laugh, so I'm filling up with petrol and watching my back. A woman on a garage forecourt, late thirties, nothing special, nothing out of the ordinary, except for the blood on my right hand and the plane ticket in my left pocket.

Like I said, appearances can be deceiving.

Sylvia Telfer, Bristol

## Big Pattie

The key was his only ally. He daren't bring anyone else in on this. The stakes were too high for any screw-ups. If he could take *this* from Big Pattie, the most evil woman in the world, he'd do kangaroo hops down the main street dressed in a tutu. She'd changed the locks a week ago but he'd had the smarts to get a copy. He was gripping the key so tightly in his palm, it bit into his flesh. A small bead of blood lay on his Mount of Venus like an evil red eye. He suspected Big Pattie of dabbling in the occult. She'd use anything to get her way. For sure, he'd have to keep a cool head.

He glanced out of his kitchen window, swilling down some morning coffee, and went over his plan. He'd sneak into Big Pattie's house at night, and take the most precious thing in the world to him. Unfortunately, it was the most precious thing in her world too.

At eight pm, he got into his car and headed off. He glanced at the petrol gauge, almost zero. He'd have to call into a petrol station. But there was ample time. He rammed the petrol nozzle hard in. He'd love to ram Big Pattie's words down her throat. The feud between them was heavy.

His belly rumbled. He glanced around. A café adjacent to the garage still had its lights on and its 'open' placard on the door.

"Hamburger with extra fries," he growled to the middle-aged blonde who'd obviously had something going with peroxide.

He glanced through the window. A Merc was pulling

up right outside the window. What the hell! It was Big Pattie. Coincidence, or was she onto him? He pulled his hat down over his eyes and made for the emergency exit.

The blonde yelled after him to pay. He retraced a few steps, tossed her a twenty dollar bill and then fled through the exit. It was so close a shave, he could smell Big Pattie's perfume. 'Poison'. She was indeed poison personified.

He pulled up outside Big Pattie's house. Inside was what he craved but, out of the corner of his eye, he saw the Merc halting a few metres down the road. Why wasn't she putting her wheels in the garage? Was she hot on his trail? At least she didn't know he was already here. She was lying in wait.

He vaulted a wall into the nearby park and moodily walked about contemplating his next move. He'd not anticipated her being around. He knew her movements. She should have been in L.A. Had someone had given the game away? Who was it? He'd played this close to his chest.

He sat down on a park bench and pulled out his notebook. He ticked the list of suspects off one by one. No one reared their head to the top of the list. He was drawing a blank. Feet on grass. Someone was near him. Had she sent one of her people? She was dangerous enough in herself. He pushed his thin frame under the park bench and covered himself with newspapers that were lying nearby.

"It's just a dosser," he heard a man's voice snarl.

"He's got be around here somewhere," Big Pattie insisted.

"He'll have high-tailed it," the man said.

"Guess you're right. He's no match for me," Big Pattie sneered.

"You're the Big Mommy in this city," the man growled.

He sounded a real heavyweight.

He looked at his watch. Almost midnight. Her Merc was no longer down the street and there were no lights on in the house. If Big Pattie was around, she'd be up until the early hours of the morning playing poker. She was an addict for poker. But he'd have to be careful.

He turned the key in the lock and slipped into the house. It was silent as the grave. The thick carpet muffled his footsteps. He knew exactly where to go. He crept up the staircase until he reached the third floor, and went to the room at the end of the corridor. He stepped inside. But what was going on? The window was wide open. Then, searing light struck his eyes.

Big Pattie was in the doorway, hands on her massive hips with two burly men behind her. He couldn't make them out because Big Pattie was BIG and she filled the room. Terror gripped him. There had been a tip-off for sure. Before, he hadn't been certain but he'd find the grass, and annihilate him or her.

Big Pattie pointed to the window.

"Out you get, buster. You stinking thief! You'll rue the day you tried to steal the most precious thing in the world to me!" she shouted.

"It belongs to me!" he shouted back.

"Cut the cackle and get out the window!" she continued to shout.

His heart tightened. It was a fifty foot drop to a concrete patio below that window.

"I'll die if I go out that window," he muttered.

She put her hand in her pocket. Something hard was inside it and she was pointing it at him through her lime velvet jacket.

"You choose," she hissed.

There was a smile on her face that would refreeze the melting polar icecaps. His brain was almost bursting but if he could catch hold of a drainpipe, he'd be able to shimmy down. It was a better chance than being blasted away.

He clambered out. Fear was a tight knot in his belly. His foot struck something. The top of a ladder! Was this one of her cruel jokes and she'd have an accomplice down below ready to yank the ladder away? He'd have to take the chance. He couldn't go back into that room and face the Evil standing there.

He clattered down the ladder, falling the last six feet. Then, he heard it. That sound! She indeed still had what he'd come for, what he desperately wanted. He risked a look up. Yes, the bitch had him. She had Charlie. He could just make out Charlie's terrified eyes. Big Pattie held Charlie aloft.

"You bastard, you think you can take Charlie from me!" she screamed.

She kicked the ladder away and he sprang to one side to avoid being struck on the head but it caught him to the side of his skull. The last thing he saw was Big Pattie holding aloft a heavy chain.

"You're the worst ex-husband in the world!" she yelled.

And the last thing he heard was Charlie yapping and growling high above him. He loved that little terrier.

Maggie Knight, Brighton

Small Pleasures


Mr Philby stood at the top of his ladder, cleaning the windows at 43 Railway Cuttings. Mr Ashcroft, who worked at the petrol station, was filling up Mrs Sanders' car and smiling at her. The tramp, Arthur, was asleep on the park bench, a newspaper laid across his face, and the train, the 5.17 that ran from the station... well, back to the station, was running on time, as it always did.

Mr Philby watched it out of the corner of his eye. He would have liked to turn his head and maybe even wave to the lady in the blue beret, who always sat in the corner seat at the back of the train, but he had to content himself with a glimpse and wonder, yet again, if she had ever noticed him. He wanted to change places with Mr Turner at the railway station, but Mr Turner said that a window cleaner wasn't a station porter and how would he like to push a trolley all day?

Of course the normal arguments had started and before everyone knew it, the key turned in the lock and it was the usual mad dash for everyone to get back in their right place before *he* noticed.

"Where do you think the train goes every evening?" Arthur asked one night.

"What do you mean, where does it go?" replied Mr Ashcroft.

"Well I've never seen it, I only hear it. I'm stuck under that paper all day."

"*He* opens the blocked-up tunnel marked 'emergency exit' where the track finishes, and puts the

69

train in there. I heard him say the door is to keep the dust out." Mr Philby answered and pushed his cloth cap back off his face. If he had to spend another day up that ladder, looking in the window in mock horror at Mr Sanders and Mrs Ashcroft, who had been having an affair for the last five years and spent their whole time in bed together... words failed him. He scratched his head and looked sad.

Arthur coughed and fiddled with the string that held his coat together.

"I've never seen the train or *him*. I'm stuck on that ruddy park bench. Hey, Mr Ashcroft, can I be the petrol attendant tomorrow? I'd be careful."

"Oh no Arthur, that wouldn't do at all." Mrs Sanders batted her baby blue eyes at him and straightened her pristine white gloves. "What would people say? What would *he* say, if he saw a tramp working at the petrol station?"

"Or a window cleaner playing at station porter! The very idea!" Mr Turner bristled, red faced, as he twiddled with his handlebar moustache and all too suddenly the key turned in the lock of the bedroom door and everyone dived for their usual places.

Mr Philby held the cloth in his hand, as if to put an extra sparkle on the window as the fluorescent lights flickered, heralding daytime, and *he* opened the door.

*He* was the boy, who took such care when he put the train on the track and dusted everyone once a week. Once he had almost left the train out for the night and Mr Philby had raced over to the station, his heart singing at the thought he would finally meet Miss Blue Beret, but the wretched key had turned in the lock again and he had spent an unpleasant half hour staring at a blank wall because he didn't have time to climb up to the right place on the ladder. The boy was a giant as he loomed over the board and its models; sometimes Mr Philby thought that Arthur was lucky, not seeing anything all day except the newsprint.

The model layout was a large one, with a long train line running through a small town, complete with shops, petrol station, a town hall, and a park. The track only ever terminated at the tunnel where the train, and Miss Blue Beret, were stored at night. There were rumours that this tunnel, labelled Emergency Exit, could be used to escape from the small world, but of course, these were only rumours.

Today was different; the boy took the train out and set the engine running. Mr Philby turned his head slightly to watch Miss Blue Beret as she whizzed by for the sixth time and wondered if she ever got dizzy.

She waved!

The next time the train came past, Mr Philby turned his head a little more and smiled. Inside the house, Mr Sanders and Mrs Ashcroft tutted in disgust, saying to each other "he'll be seen, he'll be seen". But Mr Philby didn't care, he risked a wave of his hand and even doffed his cap. That night, as soon the trains were put away and the door locked, which apparently was to keep out 'the dog', because it had once eaten someone, Mr Philby was in disgrace.

"The very idea of it, what did you think you were doing? You might have been seen!" stormed Mr Ashcroft. "We might all get found out." He turned to pat Mrs Sanders on the shoulder as she dissolved into tears. Mr Turner fiddled with his moustache and sighed heavily.

"Sometimes, I think it might be very nice to lie on a park bench all day." He looked down at his shiny black shoes as everyone turned to stare at him.

Mr Ashcroft cleared his throat awkwardly.

"Ahem… I've often wondered what it was like to be a window cleaner."

Mrs Ashcroft and Mr Sanders both blushed and said nothing. The argument raged on until the key turned in the lock again, but before anyone could say otherwise, Mr Philby raced to the railway station and stood on the platform. Arthur grinned in delight and ignored his park bench for the pleasures of the petrol pump.

Mrs Ashcroft and Mr Sanders had already disappeared inside 43 Railway Cuttings and it only took a moment's thought before Mr Ashcroft followed and climbed up the ladder outside. Mrs Sanders hesitated, then ignored her car and joined Mr Ashcroft up the ladder: she had heard the rumours for years and wanted to see for herself if it was true or not.

Mr Turner was left standing uncertainly in the town square. The park bench beckoned to him and as he ran past the railway station, he tossed his official hat to Mr Philby, who was grappling with the luggage trolley.

Mr Philby never climbed his ladder again. He was last seen sitting next to Miss Blue Beret, both of them smiling and waving farewell as the train was placed into the tunnel for the night. He was confident they were about to make their exit. Mr Ashcroft and Mrs Sanders looked through the window of 43 Railway Cuttings and decided they would divorce their partners and get married. But Arthur and Mr Turner each agreed they did not like swapping places and felt that someone should keep the status quo, as it were.

The boy looked at the railway layout. Petrol Pete and Park Bench Bob were in the wrong places and there were two figures were up the ladder. He frowned and shrugged: he was bored with the trains, and the girl who lived across the road was cute and smiled at him.

He walked out of the room, leaving the door... wide open.

Naomi Walker, Bath

## Not Even Then!

I watched my husband's expression change from anxiousness to panicked desperation. How many times had I asked him – told him – not to lock the emergency exit?

"But I always have the key on me!" He would exclaim, as if that made it any less dangerous or illegal. I cannot remember when I gave up asking what would happen to any poor souls who got trapped by fire or some such hazard if he were not with them; I might as well have been talking to the door! As a result, whenever I was not in our petrol station store, the emergency exit remained padlocked shut. Not even a hefty fine, paid by me of course, and the threat of closure could break him of his habit. The ironic sight of him now futilely tugging and shaking the chains he himself had fitted makes me laugh. This might just do it! He ignores me like I knew he would, kicking the unmoving door in terrified frustration.

It took a lot of effort on my half to ensure he picked up the correct key today. The key so identical to the original it was copied from that you could compare them with a magnifying glass and swear they were the same. The key so subtly flawed by the incompetent who cut it as to make utterly useless. The key my husband has just broken off in the lock! He sinks to his knees sobbing. I am *so* grateful he never threw it away! All the while the flames lick closer, filling the air with choking fumes. Soon he will find out for himself what would have happened to the lives he so recklessly endangered.

Watching him cry I think back to a year ago when my broken-hearted tears splashed onto the very same spot on the floor. Trying to take my husband by surprise on our anniversary I surprised myself by finding him in the storeroom with another woman. Like him I found myself trapped by his padlock when I tried to escape the scene of his crime. Clothes hastily donned he emerged to find me in the same position he now occupies. He had no apologies for me, only... "I've been meaning to tell you; I want a divorce! You can keep the house but I'm having the petrol station!" – before returning to his trollop in the stockroom.

The awkward sympathy offered by the braver of those witness to my humiliation was spittle to a forest fire. In truth it was my husband's words that soothed my grief the most. I could have the house but he was having the petrol station? Both were in my name. If he wanted the petrol station he was in for a fight! The following morning, I had the locks changed, and filed for divorce. I also instructed the solicitor of the exact words to use when informing my soon to be ex-husband the conclusion I had come to over his suggested settlement.

Terrible though the end of my marriage was, the incident that prompted the current conflagration occurred a few months later. Each month, every month throughout my marriage I had cleaned the windows of our house. This habit continued even when the marriage did not. As always I began with the upstairs windows in case any splashes or spills might dirty those below. I stood my trusty ladder on the concrete patio and started up. Soapsuds spread halfway across the master bedroom panes when the struts my husband had so carefully and invisibly sawn partially through gave way. In hindsight I can see my mistake: when I had the locks changed I failed to include those of the garage where I kept the ladder. Too late now of course! I hit the patio just milliseconds after my bucket did, but fared not nearly so well. Twelve feet may not sound a long way but it depends entirely on how you land. In the un-overlooked garden my husband had plenty of time to remove the broken ladder and replace it with an undamaged one, artfully tipped as though I had simply fallen. I watched him helplessly. Afterwards nobody listened when I told them what he had done. Oh, there was an investigation, but it was token only and he had worn gloves. My fall was deemed an accident. I was devastated. Then he was given the petrol station and I could not even appeal. That was what rankled the most! So I decided to take justice into my own hands.

Committing arson in my current condition has not been easy but I was determined. As for switching the key so my husband would burn with his prize... well, I made the extra effort for two reasons. Firstly, this way, at least I can be confident he will not rebuild, therefore the destruction does not have to be so wholesale. I worried that I might endanger innocent lives if the petrol tanks exploded. This way only the store itself, not the pumps need to burn.

And the second reason, the main reason for my husband's imminent and truly unpleasant demise? That lies half a mile away from our current location. No one would suspect it could provide the last decisive sliver of motive behind premeditated homicide. No one ever will. Above suspicion it sits by a path in the local park, and provides temporary respite for the world-weary. Only I see it for what it is; one final gesture of his contempt.

The flames have reached him now and my unfinished business is almost done. He screams a lot but I do not pity him. How could I? It was bad enough to be murdered by this man but for him to have the nerve, the shear gall, to have a park bench dedicated to me...

So now all that is left is a few last words, a belated reply to his last words to me.

"You *did* say 'over your dead body!'"

How could he be so stupid? I'm sure he should know, like every one else, those four little words translate into just three.

'Not even then!'

Nik Morton, Alicante, Spain


## Lucky with cars


Twenty miles after I'd left home, the petrol gauge needle was hovering over the red. My green Ford Escort was just running on the fumes in the tank when I breasted the hill. Yes! My luck was still holding. At the bottom of the slope was a garage. I coasted down and turned in to the forecourt, a smug grin on my face. My wife Maureen was forever telling me off for letting the tank get too low. 'One of these days, you'll get stranded! And I don't want to be sitting here with you when it happens!'

She wasn't, fortunately, or else I'd have received an ear-pounding for the last five miles or so. Still, I got to the petrol station, didn't I? I had never cut it so fine, though.

I recalled that time when my old Austin's accelerator pedal jammed. That was scary! I'd take it out of gear and brake but the engine continued to rev. Deafening. As I was driving through country lanes, I didn't want to risk switching off the engine. So I revved on till I found a garage. I received a few weird looks as I pulled in. The owner lifted the bonnet and used his air hose to clean the gubbins inside. "Clogged with dirt," he said. Sorted. Nice bloke.

I ignored the knocking near the rear axle.

And one Saturday, when my exhaust fell off, I kept going. The Noise Abatement Society didn't exist then. Maybe I was the reason they started up. Anyway, I found one of the few garages open and they had a suitable exhaust. Lucky with cars, that's me.

But not this time.

As I braked alongside the pumps, I realised that the garage was closed.

My heart sank.

I wasn't a member of any motoring organisation; I thought that with my good luck, I didn't need one. My mate Alan said they didn't take too kindly to people running out of petrol, anyway.

Nothing for it, then. I would have to telephone Alan.

But the telephone kiosk had been vandalised. It was times like this when I wished I could afford a mobile phone. Maureen said we should both get one. Keep in touch. I'd probably let the battery run down and it would cut out at a vital part of a conversation.

I left a note in the car's windscreen to explain that there was no need to worry, I wasn't a terrorist or anything. Then I started walking back towards town.

At least it was a summer evening. As dusk fell, I could see clearly where I was going. I tried thumbing a lift a couple of times, but nobody stopped. I wouldn't have, either. Not these days. You don't know who you'll pick up.

According to the road signs and my aching feet, I must have walked twelve miles. Here, on the outskirts of town was a park named after some Marxist African, complete with benches and roses and trees. The roses reminded me of Maureen – not their scent but the thorn in my side. The park bench was most welcome as I sat down to rest my feet. Only a minute or two then I would get going again, crack the final eight miles.

I must have slept and woke an hour later, shivering with dew on my face. I couldn't remember the last time I'd been walking the streets at such an unsocial hour. Maureen would have been livid, if she'd known.

Two hours later I got to our street and quickened my pace and opened the front gate. It creaked. Maureen was always on to me to get it oiled. As I stood in the porch and fished in my pockets, I realised that I had dropped my keys somewhere. Probably in the park when I was asleep.

What a night this was turning out to be!

Walking round the side of our house, I scuffled past the wheelie-bin and reached up over the edge of the wood-panelled gate. Hanging on a piece of string was the key. I opened the gate. I hadn't fancied climbing over. The way things had been going tonight, I'd probably have slipped and broken my neck. Serves you right, Maureen would have said.

At the bottom of the garden was my shed, my final refuge from Maureen, and screwed above the door was an old sign I had pinched from a demolished building: EMERGENCY EXIT. Maureen never got the joke. My ladder hung on the side of the shed; I never bothered to padlock it though Maureen reckoned I should have, otherwise I was making it easy for burglars. Now, I was glad I hadn't listened to her.

Lifting the ladder to the back of our house, I rested it against the wall.

Our bathroom window was always left open. Maureen liked the fresh air. Even in the height of winter. I just shivered and kept quiet.

As I struggled to get my thin body through the window, I swore a few times. I'd wanted to leave a spare key under the gnome but Maureen had vetoed that.

Finally, after jamming my left foot in the lavatory pan and barking my shin on the bidet – Maureen again, she wanted it to match our jacuzzi – I was inside my home at last.

Limping downstairs, I left a wet footprint as I went. My spare car keys were in the lounge bureau and I found Maureen's keys in the kitchen drawers, suitably labelled: 'My keys. Do not use!'

Sorry, old girl, I thought, needs must.

Our lockup was at the end of the street and her Morris 1000 was in pristine condition, a collector's item. It should be, she got me to polish it twice a week. She drove it only on Sundays, to visit her sister.

I quite enjoyed driving it. Devilment almost tempted me to nudge the odd bollard here and there.

By now I was having difficulty keeping my eyes open. Mustn't wander across the road. Have an accident. Not now.

It was amazing how quickly I got back to the garage.

As I pulled in behind my car I popped the boot of the Morris.

I got out and unlocked my Escort's boot. I'd transfer Maureen to the Morris. Quicker. I lifted the boot and stared.

It was empty.

"Having a problem, sir?"

I swung round and two policemen were standing on the forecourt. One of them switched on a torch and shone the beam in my eyes.

"No, officer," I said, which was quite untrue.

When did she get out? I'd heard her knocking as I reached the brow of the hill...

"If you're looking for your wife, sir, she's quite safe in the hospital," said the policeman with the torch. "While on patrol we saw your car stranded here and stopped to investigate."

I listened, quite numb.

He went on, "We read your note and were about to leave when your wife's knocking against the boot alerted us." He shrugged. "I think you can help us with our enquiries, sir."

If only I had listened to Maureen and made sure that I'd had a full tank!

Jenna Pogue, Coventry

## No place like home

"Betty, look at that. What a disgrace!"

I turned to see an elderly couple approaching, their faces distorted with disgust. As I moved, the splintered wood of the park bench tore through my tatty jumper and into my shoulder. Twisting in pain, I longed for my warm bed, for the buzz of my wife's alarm clock that used to wake me. The wind and rain are my alarm now, raising me from a derelict doorway or a park bench.

I watched the pair speed away, arms linked and looking back nervously, as if they wouldn't be safe until I was out of sight. The sting in my shoulder became insignificant as shame stole my thoughts, bringing more pain than any sharp object could inflict. I'm just another homeless tramp to them.

They don't know of the nice life and loving family that redundancy and my wife's infidelity robbed me of last year. They don't know how feelings of failure engulfed me when my wife threw me out. Or the anguish I felt seeing my teary-eyed children banging on the window as I left. Or how fury erupted when I returned weeks later, newly employed and hoping to start again, to find another man on my sofa.

Today was bin day and with hunger competing with shame over which was more unbearable I found myself rummaging through an overflowing bin. Jagged cans grazed my skeletal wrists and broken glass pierced beneath my fingernails like torture devices. Turning away to avoid the stench I saw a glint of metal at my feet. I prayed it was money. It was a car key. My urge to kick the fence in frustration was great until an even stronger urge crept in. One I'd wrestled with repeatedly since becoming homeless. It was easy to fight at first, when I believed I'd be back on track before long. The uncaring passage of time proved me wrong. The determination I once relied on was replaced by a demon on my shoulder telling me the only way to save myself now was to steal.

I was three miles away before I considered what was happening. I hadn't wanted to take the car. I didn't want to drive to a rough side of town and sell it. I don't want to become the type of person that I resent existing in the same world as my children.

Being in a car was a long forgotten luxury; I'm amazed I even remembered how to drive. The streets have left me feeble.

A flash of red on the control panel pushed any humiliation to the back of my mind. The petrol was low. Fumbling anxiously around the glove box for spare change I saw a £5 note appear from between some papers. I'd already stolen the car, a few pounds were inconsequential now.

Driving into the bad side of town, I saw homeless people everywhere. Those who were still sober stared in irritation at the expensive car trespassing on their territory, unaware the driver was no better off than them. Pulling into a ramshackle petrol station I felt torn. Should I just leave the car and take the money? Should I leave the money as well?

A tiny slice of my old self prevailed. I'd return the car. I needed to clear my mind first; I needed air. Stepping onto the forecourt I felt relief until a clattering of metal put me back on edge. I spun around to see a van charging forwards. A paint-stained ladder clung loosely to its roof; a piece of thin blue rope fighting to restrain it. As the van swerved past, the ladder swung violently sideways and dug deep into my face. There wasn't time to feel pain as the force sent me hurtling into a pit of darkness.

A powerful voice revived me. Desperate to see where I was and who was with me, I forced my eyes open against the weight of pain bearing down on them. I regretted it instantly as light burned through, sending waves of pain across my skull. Amongst the hazy images one unmistakable vision emerged: a burly policeman stood ahead, side-on to me. I quickly closed my eyes again before he saw, and played dead.

"Sir, are you sure you don't know this man? Or why he was driving your car?"

"I'm sure."

"And you're certain you didn't give him permission to take the car for any reason?"

"Officer, he stole it. Look at him, he's obviously a criminal!"

"OK, but there's nothing we can do until he regains consciousness. Go home and we'll be in touch soon. My colleague's in the nurse's office, let me show you where and she'll take your contact details. Don't worry; he won't get away with it."

I tugged my legs from under the blanket and swung them over the edge of the bed. My vision was fuzzy but I could see that none of the nurses were paying attention. I had to get out.

The effort of getting up throbbed through me. A wave of nausea propelled me forward while searing pains almost brought me back down. Holding the bed for stability, I fought my way to the door. Just a few steps. I made them quickly, fighting against the pain and praying I wouldn't fall.

Down the corridor I saw the police officer beside the door. I looked the other way. An emergency exit. My last chance. I stumbled towards it, looking over my shoulder in fear of being caught. As the cold metal bar met my hands I turned in relief to see the bright green emergency exit. The intense block of colour stung my eyes but I didn't care. I was free. Taking the deepest breath I could, I focused my flagging energy on the door. The ease with which it opened stunned me and I stumbled. The yell of the policeman forced me upright as my legs fought for freedom.

Crouching behind an old skip, the policeman out of sight, I felt relief. I was safe. Until a broken mirror in the skip caught my reflection and I realised something. I'm not safe: I'm not safe from the life of despair that I'm falling into.

Digging deep into my pocket for a tissue I found the £5 note from earlier. I stared at it, not sure what to do. I was starving; I could get something to eat. Or I could just give in to the pull of the street and get a bottle of cheap cider. I was torn for what felt like the hundredth time that day until the tattered face in the mirror told me what to do. In a nearby shop I bought two small envelopes and a pencil, then headed towards my old street.

Standing on the doorstep I thought about my future. For the first time in months I vowed to have one. I wasn't sure how I'd get there or what kind of a future it'd be but I was determined to make it one my daughters could be proud of. I pushed the envelopes towards the letterbox; two coins rattled inside each one.

I read the words scribbled on the front one more time before committing them to the doormat.

'Love from Daddy.'

Kate Greagsby, Blyth

Love was the key

Nadine sat in her favourite thinking place, on the lone park bench under the lengthening, sharpened evening shadows.

The forthcoming night's chill settled to sleep across her back and shoulders as she fingered again the cold key in the pocket of her thin jacket. The key! The one she'd found on her bedroom carpet. The tell-tale key that had slipped from her husband's trouser pocket the night before.

Two thoughts occurred: one; it wasn't *her* bedroom carpet, alone, per se. It belonged equally to Nadine and her husband, Tim. And two; Tim's trouser department was another affair altogether! Something that didn't belong solely to Nadine – Tim being her husband notwithstanding!

She knew exactly where the key belonged, whose key it was. That bitch hairdresser on Lansdowne Terrace, Michelle – 'Ma Belles'.

The words of the Beatles' song tortured her brain.

Three simple words, I love you, once whispered softly at one side of a marriage contract, now screamed at the other – only, in another's ear.

Well, he could have his Mee-chelle. She'd caught them in cahoots several times on her way back from lunch to the bank on Lansdowne Terrace where she worked, only three doors away from 'Ma Belles', the hairdressers.

She recalled the last time she'd seen Tim coming out of there; how he'd spotted her, Nadine, coming out of the bank, and how quickly he'd dived back into the shop. By the time Nadine had reached the hairdressers and looked in, Tim was nowhere to be seen, having obviously escaped through the emergency exit at the back of the shop.

How sordid and tawdry was that! And Mee-chelle *still* had the nerve to wave at Nadine as she passed. The bitch! Nadine had blanked her. She was welcome to Tim. With knobs on!

The unfortunate allusion might once have brought a wry smile to Nadine's face, but not now her heart was hurting so.

Darkness began to descend, and instinctive survival pulled Nadine from the park bench. It was time to go home. Home... Ha! Such as it was. 'Home is where the heart is'... or was.

As she walked past the flower beds Nadine smelled their perfume, sharpened in the chill night air. Twenty yards from the park gates she became aware of the voices ahead of her, just outside the park: male voices, one raised and angry, the other calm and appeasing.

Nadine stepped quickly from the path onto the grass to quieten her footsteps and slowed her pace. If there was a fight brewing ahead she didn't want to step into the middle of it.

She could barely make out Mr. Calm's voice, soothing:

"Now come on, you don't know that for sure, she might not be."

Nadine had no such trouble with Mr. Angry's voice as it boomed like thunder on the night air, stopping Nadine in her tracks:

"I tell you, she's moved back into her flat above the hairdressers. I bet she's there with him right now!"

Nadine, heart racing, ran for cover behind the large

oak tree just behind the park gates, and listened.

Mr. Calm: "Look, Dave, I don't think Michelle's the type to run around."

So it *was* Mee-chelle they were talking about! And her Tim the one she was running around with. Nadine had even found his suitcase half packed.

She was briefly tempted to step out from cover and declare herself: That's my husband you're talking about. But Mr. Angry – 'Dave' – boomed again.

"Look – if you don't want to *take* me, I'll walk there, myself!"

With that Mr. Angry stormed off and, peeping around the tree, Nadine caught a glimpse of 'Dave'. A big bloke in a black and yellow hooped rugby shirt, he was like a huge, angry wasp.

Nadine heard Mr. Calm's footsteps retreating in the opposite direction, watched him get into a car and drive off.

With the coast clear, she left the park and got into her own car. When she came to the crossroads, instead of turning left for home, she turned right. She kidded herself that it was to fill the car up with petrol, but even as she filled the tank she knew exactly where she was heading.

It was a little after 10 pm when she stood outside 'Ma Belles' looking up at the flat above the hairdressers. It was in darkness.

A sudden strange honking sound drew Nadine's attention to the night sky above the building and against the blackness she made out the figure of a lone swan. Unusual to see a lone swan in flight, Nadine reflected, and was suddenly filled with as much pity for the creature as for herself. Maybe the swan was going home, which is what she should have done. What on earth was she doing here? What had she hoped to achieve?

She felt for the key in her jacket pocket and flung it with all her spite into the large rhododendron bush in front of 'Ma Belles' window.

Even if Nadine had driven up the back lane behind the hairdressers, she wouldn't have seen the huge, angry wasp up a ladder trying to break in, for the tears stinging her eyes.

By the time she reached home her tears had been replaced by resolve: to go in, lock the door and bolt it. No way was he getting in tonight. She'd think about his half-packed suitcase in the morning, maybe leave it out on the doorstep. Right now, she planned to get drunk.

Pouring her fourth glass of wine, Nadine didn't hear the footfalls coming down the stairs, or the door into the living room open. She only heard the familiar voice.

"Where've you been till this time?"

Nadine spun round, spilling wine on the carpet.

"I'll get a cloth," Tim said. "I've waited so long I fell asleep on the bed."

Nadine tried to shake the alcoholic haze from her brain.

Tim returned with the cloth and started scrubbing the carpet.

"Well?"

"Well what?" Nadine could barely speak.

"Where've you been till now?"

Where've *I* been? What've *you* been up to and who with, more like! The words didn't actually form in Nadine's mouth. She could only glare at her husband as he continued to scrub the carpet. When was he planning to tell her?

As though reading her thoughts, Tim stopped scrubbing and looked directly into Nadine's eyes.

"The thing is, Nade, I've gotta come clean about

something. You know Michelle, the hairdresser...?"

Nadine stiffened. So this was it then, the end of her marriage.

Tim's voice became alien to her as he continued.

"Well, you know that holiday cottage she had up in Kippford, the one you always loved...? She'd put it up for sale, and so well... I hope you don't mind, but I've bought it for you. I was planning to take us there tomorrow for a long weekend, but the stupid thing is, Nade, I've gone and lost the key..."

Caroline Carter, Cheltenham

<u>The Doctor's Ladder</u>

Peter sat at his hospital desk. Too numb to cry he just cradled his head in hands, disbelieving. The grief inside him was overwhelming but as yet could not erupt.

He thought back over the events of the previous evening. They were vivid in his mind.

He remembered climbing that ladder, at the time asking himself what in heaven's name he was doing – had he gone completely crazy? He could be risking everything, his job, his marriage, his reputation.

Climbing ladders wasn't something he was used to, even less so in the dark, and he trembled as he climbed. No, ladders didn't feature much in his life. Being a senior doctor always on the go and working hours on end, he preferred to pay for painters, decorators, window cleaners and roofers to do any ladder work needed on his house.

As he had tentatively moved from rung to rung he felt nervous – frightened – yet the thought of what lay ahead brought an excitement that he had not felt for years and years.

He had been honest from the start. As he and Lucy sat on the hospital bench earlier that day (it was several months ago on that same bench, genuinely discussing work, that the chemistry had first reared its head) he had made no pretence. He would never leave his wife of thirty years – his childhood sweetheart. They were devoted, the perfect couple. Until now he had been a man of the highest principles. Never had he cheated, flirted nor even looked at any other woman. He loved his wife. Unfortunately he loved Lucy too: it wasn't lust, it was love – of that there was no doubt. Twenty-five years his junior, he must be off his head.

As he had climbed the ladder he asked himself again, what *was* he doing? Falling for a student nurse, sneaking into her place the back way for fear of being seen by the neighbours. The row of small terraced houses was mainly occupied by other student doctors and nurses.

Shaking, half from fear, half from excitement, he managed to push up the sash window. It needed attention, the sill was rotting. He thought of his own recently replaced PVC windows in his executive 5 bed house with its 2 acre garden.

He breathed a sigh of relief as he finally scrambled through the window in a most inelegant fashion. At least the ladder had not disappeared from under his feet.

As he entered the back bedroom he dared not switch on the light. A little lamp had been lit ready, throwing out a cosy warmth amidst the student décor and muddle. It was then that he noticed the sign Lucy had strung up above the window. Emergency Exit! One of those green things that were everywhere in public buildings. He laughed, wondering where she had picked that up from, preferring not to know. This would not be his idea of a quick exit.

His mobile rang. It was Lucy.

"You made it then!" she giggled. "I'm just at the petrol station, I'll be back in a few minutes. Do you want a choccy bar?" she asked childishly.

He smiled with affection as he remembered it all.

Ten minutes later the key turned in the lock. He had told her that he never wanted a key, he didn't want the temptation of being able to let himself in whenever he felt like it, and he didn't want the risk of ever being seen entering. Tonight was a one-off. Workmen had been working on the brickwork and the ladder was an opportune aid. It was just 'one of those nights'.

There had followed the most fantastic evening, only spoilt by the fact that he had had to leave prematurely due to being on call and the undignified fashion in which he had exited.

He remembered it all so well. As he shook his head between his hands, tears began to well, emotion rising to the surface.

It had been around 11 that morning, when the news broke. After an exhausting night, first at Lucy's and then at the operating theatre, he was in the staff canteen, taking a much needed cappuccino. Surrounded by some of his trainee doctors they were mulling over the emergency operation.

He couldn't even remember now exactly what had been said, but the news of the murder was a shock to all. Even those who didn't know the victim, those to whom she was just an anonymous workmate, were stunned. In their job they were used to trauma and horrifying events but things like this didn't happen to normal people around you.

The first rumours filtered through; details were sparse and information half concocted. Yet Peter froze. He knew at once. It wasn't the name, there was no name to begin with. It was the mention of the ladder.

A young girl, attacked by someone who had climbed the ladder. An abandoned ladder against a wall. The perfect opportunity for a madman, a sick and violent lowlife.

It was terrible. It was unbearable. Firstly the crime itself, the horror of what had happened to Lucy, the tragedy, the waste of life, the injustice of it.

Then there was Peter's grief. He had done wrong and

perhaps it served him right, but that didn't alter his anguish. And the worst was the inability to share it with anybody. To all the others, he was just an impartial doctor, sad and sorry of course like all staff, shocked and aghast, with sympathy for the girl's family, but nothing more, nothing special; no personal grief could be afforded to him. How could he ever continue as normal, how could he hide the emotions, the turmoil within? How would he hide his misery from his workmates, his seniors, his trainees, his wife?

There was worse to come. As 'luck' would have it, one of the young doctors on Peter's shift had a brother who worked in the local CID. Apparently oblivious to the Official Secrets Act that he must have once signed, he imparted information to his brother who then did the same to Peter. Perhaps it was a young lad's way of impressing his peers or his seniors. It transpired that a key had been left on the floor next to the bedside table. It wasn't a key that fitted any doors of the victim's house. Of course, it had been seized as forensic evidence. Peter was well aware that on that fateful visit, the key to his own house had dropped out of his trouser pocket and in his haste, he had forgotten to retrieve it. It seemed so unimportant at the time. Lucy would bring it to him the following day.

As the snippets of gruesomeness trickled through, fuelling the interest of some of the less savoury characters, feeding their thirst for the macabre, Peter wondered what evidence might be linked to him?

There was more to come. The poor assaulted girl would be undergoing tests. All the usual bodily secretions would remain for analysis and all the hospital staff were to be tested too.

Yes, he had done wrong, but his crime was not that of murder.

Joss Hayes, Middlesbrough

<u>Mum</u>

Last year my mother fell off her roller skates and broke her arm. If I were six years old, people might be a little surprised by that information, but would assume my mother to be young and fit. I'm not six. In a matter of months I'll be collecting my senior citizens' bus pass.

I received a phone call from the sports centre – would I come pronto, as my mother had had a little accident, not serious, but somebody would need to accompany her to the hospital. When I turned up, she was sitting quite cheerfully in the staff room, her arm in a makeshift sling, waiting for the ambulance to arrive.

"You fell off what?!" I asked incredulously.

"They did warn me," she said a little sheepishly. "I had to sign a bit of paper to say I would learn at my own risk. They told me bones the age of mine are fragile. Not that fragile really or I'd have broken more than my arm," she laughed somewhat painfully.

As the ambulance men carried her out through the emergency exit, she was at pains to explain to them that the whole episode was part of her new philosophy – to experience as much as possible in what was left of her life.

Last month I had another call, the police this time. Would I please come and see to my mother. I tried to tell them that as my mother was a grown woman in her right mind, she should see to herself, but they weren't prepared to accept the 'right mind' bit. She was lying on a park bench, head on a cushion, wrapped in the multi-coloured crochet blanket usually draped over the back seat of her car. She was refusing to move on or go home. It was two in the morning. When I arrived she was deep in an attempt to explain her philosophy to two baffled young bobbies.

"Seems she means to experience homelessness. If she insists on staying here, she'll wind up experiencing hypothermia."

"Mum," I pleaded. "Enough is enough. Let's take you home."

"No! I'm spending the night on a park bench. I want to know what it's like."

"OK. How about a compromise. I'll take you home with me, but you can sleep on the bench in the garden. How about that?"

She consented reluctantly.

The next morning I discovered the real reason behind her odd behaviour. I took her a cup of tea in the garden at seven, and wondered if now she'd experienced a night's homelessness, she would like to avail herself of the home she actually possessed. "There's the rub, dear," she shivered into the duvet I hadn't permitted her to go without. "I dropped the house key down a hole on the garage forecourt last night when I was refuelling. The boy behind the glass seemed to think he was endangered by me, so he just shrugged at my predicament. He wouldn't come out. The park bench idea came to me as a sort of opportunism. I'm glad I did it, anyway. Life only goes on while you keep up the new experiences."

"What next?" I wondered as I bundled her into my car and ferried her to the petrol station to retrieve her car and hopefully her key. (I do have a duplicate, had she not, by the time I appeared, been determined on sleeping rough.)

I found out what next this morning. Once again I received a call from the police. They'd had Mum in the station overnight. They'd picked her up at midnight, breaking and entering, would you believe. She was arrested half way up a ladder, trying to enter the bathroom window of a neighbour's house.

"Another new experience," was all she'd offer as an excuse. "These nice policemen have proposed a trade – one new experience for another. They refused to let me complete my burglary, but gave me a night in the cells instead. Aren't they dears?"

John Kent, Blackpool


Unfair Cop


It was gone nine when he nabbed me shimmying down the ladder.

"Serve 'em right – leaving a ladder in the front garden," I protested.

"And that's your defence, is it?" he said.

"It's like enticement. Ain't hardly a fair cop, is it?"

"Save it for the magistrate, sunshine. You're nicked."

It was when he dragged me off to his car that he discovered his keys were missing. He's pretty certain they must have fallen out of his pocket when he was chasing me. I thought it was worth doing a runner even if I am as fast as a three-legged tortoise.

So, having to hunt for them in the dark, he doesn't want to be hampered by me. Looking about, his eyes eventually settled on a park bench on the edge of the common about fifty yards away. That's how I came to be cuffed to it. He also decided it would be more effective if he shackled me by the ankle rather than my wrist.

He gave up after half an hour. He was in no hurry to admit that he was locked out of his car. That's when he found that the battery in his radio was flat.

"Not your night," I chirped.

He scowled at me then said, "I'm going back to the phone box to call for help. You stay here."

Stay here? No, officer, I'm going to hop down the high street towing a park bench.

He's no sooner out of sight than along come Alfie and Jed. Bit like the odd couple, these two. Alfie is pretty sharp, big strapping bloke. Jed's a different tale. Weedy and only knitting on one needle. Still, he's a good enough mate.

If they look a bit puzzled when they see me stretched out on a park bench at ten o'clock at night, that was nothing compared to their reaction when I showed them my ankle cuffed to the backrest.

When they had finished peeing their pants at my expense I told them to get me out of here before the cavalry comes.

"Have you got the key?" asked Jed.

"Course I have. The copper tucked it in my pocket for safekeeping, you bleedin' dunce," I snarled.

"All right, no need to get the hump," said Jed.

"Any ideas?" asks Alfie.

Good question.

"You'll just have to carry me, the bench as well."

Their look was one that provoked real pity in me.

"What choice is there?" I asked. "Unless you reckon on leaving me here."

"How can we do that, Charlie?" said Alfie. "These benches are bolted to the floor."

Jed walked down to the nearby crossroads to keep an eye out. Alfie examined the backrest but decided it was too sturdy to break. He then turned his attention to the floor bolts.

"Hey, Jed," he called, "give us a hand." He turned to me. "This looks a bit worm-eaten. I reckon if we rock it hard enough it should break out."

"Well, hurry up," I rasped.

Taking hold of the back at each end they started shoving the bench backwards and forwards. A bit tight at first then it started to give. Soon it was rocking good and I had to hold on tight. Next thing I heard was the sound of ripping wood and me and my chaise-longue ended arse-up on the pavement.

"Hell, careful," I yelled. "Quick, let's get going."

"Blimey Charlie," Jed grunted at me as he tried to lift the bench. "Can't you give a hand?"

"Yeah, Jed. Help me on my feet! Gawd, Alfie, how do you put up with him?"

"Will you two stop cribbing at each other? Now, which way?"

"Cut across the common. It's dark there. If the rozzers turn up they won't see us."

Alfie grabbed one end and Jed got the back end. We haven't gone fifty yards before Jed was struggling, running like a penguin with a crutch. He dropped his end with a thud.

"Hold on, I need a break," he wheezed.

I spotted a flashing blue light in the distance. "Look, the boys in blue are back. Just a bit further and they won't be able to see us."

With a groan they heaved the bench off the grass and wobbled further off into the darkness.

"What now then?" said Alfie.

"I've got to find a way to get rid of these cuffs."

"We need a hacksaw," said Alfie.

"I haven't got one of those," said Jed.

"Now what have I told you about leaving it at home?"

Before Jed could react I interrupted. "That's a good idea. The garage – on Raleigh Street. There's bound to be one in their workshop."

"It'll be closed," said Jed.

"We're not going for a tank of unleaded, you pillock," I said. Then, "When has a locked door ever stopped you anyway?"

True. Not a lock of any sort can keep that man out.

"Jeez, Charlie, that's nearly half a mile away."

"Well, Jed, I've got one at home. That's only three miles."

"Come on, Jed. Best foot forward," said Alfie.

With lots of rest and even more foul language we eventually got to the garage.

"Round the back," I whispered. "There's an emergency exit. I've been in there once before. It's got a bog-standard lock. Real easy pickings, Jed."

He was still puffing like Thomas the Tank but managed a weak smile. "I'd rather try to open Fort Knox with a tin opener than pick this effing bench up again," he growled.

Just our luck that the door had been changed. Must have been something to do with their insurance. There was no keyhole to pick.

"What now?" asked Alfie.

"What about using the bench as a battering ram," suggested Jed.

I did mention his quick mind didn't I? Saying nothing I looked around then spotted a small window about ten feet up.

"If we can get you up there, could you get through that window, Jed?"

"Easy peasy," he said.

I explained. With me hanging on they up-ended the bench against the wall. Alfie then gave Jed a leg up. The bench wiggled a few times before he gave a satisfied grunt then dragged himself through the small window. A minute later and I was ferried into the garage. A pair of bolt croppers was soon found. One snip and the cuffs were off.

It is just possible a good brief could have got me off through lack of evidence. When PC Jones had first chased me I had thrown my booty and I am bright enough not to leave my prints around. What did it for me was taking the bench back to the common. Well, we could hardly leave it in the garage as proof of our break-in.

I guess it was inevitable that some nosy bleeder would call the busies. Well, how often do you see three blokes carrying a park bench down the street after midnight?

Felicity Bloomfield, Canberra, Australia

Annabel's Secret

I gave up a baby girl in high school. My grief manifested in a compulsive need to keep emergency exits within my view. Irrationally, they represented freedom to me, and hope. When the service station where I worked was rearranged, the neat green sign was behind the counter. That niggled.

The new layout was a pathetic attempt to attract customers. My boss brought in flashier billboards, and she made us staffies change them weekly. We left the ladder out, leaning against the front of the shop – the Health & Safety aspect of it maddened her, but she lost the moral high ground when a customer was so enthralled by the new advertising that he crashed into a streetlight.

On breaks I walked to the park. No one went there – the grass was haphazard at best and the memorial bench cracked and dry from lack of paint. I'd bought the bench myself in year nine.

Annabel was sitting on it the first time we met, at night.

"Shouldn't you be going home?" I said.

She cringed away.

"That's my bench," I explained.

"I didn't know," she said, "I'm dense." She was wearing a bulky school jumper despite the warmth, and a key on a string around her neck. "Sorry, um, Helen."

It was my turn to cringe. She'd read the plaque. "I'm Maya. Helen... died before she was born. She'd be your age."

"Are you angry at me?"

"You've done nothing wrong."

"I do things wrong all the time."

"Oh, me too," I said, beginning to wonder about the schoolgirl's home life. "Just ask my boss."

She smiled, a glimmer on a pixie face.


I saw Annabel most days between three and seven at night, always in that jumper. One day I messed with the heating before going to the park and bringing her back to the servo. My ploy worked without a word spoken, and she finally took it off.

"What's your key for?" I said, giving no sign I'd seen the bruises on her arms.

"My diary."

"What do you write about?"

She shrugged. "Dense stuff."

"I bet it's not dense at all."

She shrugged again, looking at the ground. "Not even daddy's allowed to read it."

"Your father reads your diary?"

For the third time, she put me off with a shrug. "He lost his job last month. Sometimes he goes into my room when I'm not there."

"What else does he do?"

She met my eye. "Nothing."


Whenever she left, work was miserable.

"Why do petrol prices rise quickly in a crisis, and stay high when crises are over?" That day's irate customer wore a tailored suit, thinning from overuse.

"Actually, we're in danger of closing," I smiled brightly.

Others in the line began muttering about oil barons. I rated them five on my bad customer scale – irrational, but not violent. It could be worse. Soon it was.

The following week, Annabel was with me when two customers came in. Balaclavas made them an instant nine on the customer scale. I shoved her close to the counter and down.

"Got a safe?" said one balaclava. I recognised the crumpled and thinning suit, but didn't say anything.

"Yes, sir, out the back." My knee was touching the dial.

He made a new bad customer record by waving a firearm. "I'm not here to hurt anyone, right? The gun's for the man, not for you."

I could hear Annabel breathing.

"Sir, you should fetch the money yourself, or I'll look like an accomplice."

"You trying to be a hero?" he said.

"No sir. I hate my job, sir, but I need to keep it."

The two conferred. Suit-man stayed while the other began searching the back room. The suit strayed to the doorway while keeping an eye out.

"Annabel," I whispered. "Do you see the exit sign behind me?"

"Yes." It was barely a breath of air.

Outside was tarmac in all directions. There was only one possible hiding place. "When I tell you, go out that door and crawl to the front of the shop. Climb up the ladder and hide on the roof."

"What about daddy? That's his voice."

I flinched in sudden understanding. "He won't see you. I promise."

Her father walked into the staff room to berate his friend.

"Go now, Annabel. Quickly."

She crawled from my feet without a sound.

Moments later the men gave up. The gun turned on me. "Are you trying to make me get angry?"

"I... here. The safe is here."

"It's not enough," he said. "The servo has to burn. We're protesting petrol prices, right? Tell people that." Behind him I saw Annabel's hands on the ladder. "You have matches, right? Don't tell me you're dense enough to lie again."

"No sir." Insane or otherwise, I had to keep them facing me. Matches were under the front windows, where Annabel's knees were now exactly at eye level. She had navy stockings, and black buckled shoes. I slammed my hand onto the register, and it popped open. "While you're here..."

I emptied the safe too. The men didn't notice Annabel's schoolbag, pushed out from the wall by the emergency exit door. By the time I stood again, she was safe. Her father took the money, and matches, and piled sale price kindling around the pumps. He tied me to the dented streetlight before helping his friend douse the shop in petrol. Fires were everywhere when they walked away with two full jerrycans each.

Annabel couldn't come down until her father was gone. I longed for a customer as flames brightened the shop and curled up the walls. The front of the roof caved and our ladder fell into the hole. Annabel's tiny figure was a ghost in the smoke. She couldn't get down, and the pumps were going to explode any moment. I tugged every which way at my ropes. Salvation came as I gouged my arm. Our customer's crash had bent the streetlight into a sharp edge. I worked twice as hard, and screamed out that I was coming. My fingers were bleeding before I was free, and I ran to Annabel as fast as I could. The ladder was burning hot but I pulled and kicked at it, propping it up to the last place I'd seen her.

"Annabel! Are you there?"

Tears made tracks on her cheeks as she crouched above me. She climbed down carefully on the hot metal. Before she reached the ground I caught her. I ran to Helen's bench and safety with Annabel wrapped in my arms.

"I left my bag," she said.

"Me too." We laughed crazily until the pumps exploded. Fire shot above the trees.

"Am I in trouble?" said Annabel.

"No, but your father is."

He was convicted of several offences, most of which were meticulously recorded in Annabel's locked diary. When I asked her mum if I could visit, she appointed me as babysitter.

The servo was boarded up, with barriers around the craters where customers once pumped petrol. I found the warped exit sign when the police let me look for my things. For a moment I held it in my hands. Then I threw it away.

Eleanor Smith, Weymouth

## Age Attack

Elsie Jones was drooling again, sitting in her chair gazing at the window waiting for the sun to strike the carpet. Every day her hands twitched as the curtains were opened and the murky light through the net curtains gave an approximation of daylight. This was the most animated she was all day.

The circle of chairs facing the television was only half full today. Not all were like Elsie; one or two carried on a desultory conversation, watched the droning TV or clicked the knitting needles that seemed to grow from the folds of their voluminous clothes, remnants of a past life when woollen garments were needed. May was one of these, still quite alert with her knees swollen and painful.

She had not been there long, finding the long quiet afternoons swelling into weeks and spilling over into her dreams. Sometimes in those dreaming moments she heard her past life happen around her, kettles whistling, husband calling, children crying, doorbells ringing, and then she came back to the reality of querulous tones, groans, snores and the constant burble of television creating an artificial life sound, a pacifier for the elderly.

May had become friendly with Mr Harvey. A powerful figure in his former life but now diminished by age and circumstance. Every so often he retained a semblance of his former persona, frightening even the most familiar of nurses into some kind of politeness. Then his body let him down, emotions overcoming him in a kind of leaking of bodily fluids, from eyes, mouth and more embarrassing regions. The nurses resumed their patronising patter and his moment of normality was gone.

May and Mr Harvey had discussed the weather to start with, then the television presenters, then they started to call the residents by nicknames. Elusive Elsie, Moaning Mary, Sleeping Sidney and so on. The nurses and social workers had similar nicknames: Kind Karen, Nasty Nerys, and for one particularly officious auxiliary, The General. Mr Harvey told May about his late wife and his Labrador Henry. After his wife died the dog was his life. He and Henry went every day to the park near his house where he would sit on the same park bench and Henry would run, later plod, around the grass.

May too went to the same park as him although they had not known each other then. She went for the company, sitting watching the children play in the paddling pool in the summer. Often a harassed mother would come and chat to her, exclaiming as her lively child splashed and cavorted, but glad to have a gentle conversation with the pleasant old woman.

Twice a week a well-meaning volunteer called Lucy came to listen to their stories. She was taking part in a project to record old people's memories and May and Mr Harvey were more than happy to chat. She became very fond of the old people and her soft heart bled as they told her how they longed to see the park again. When she suggested it to the nurses they dismissed the idea as out of the question.

Lucy was having a spot of trouble of her own. With middle age well set in she could see her own future only too clearly in the old folk she went to see. She lived alone with her cat in a small flat quite close to the old folk's home and had been behaving strangely for some time now, but living alone meant that nobody was around to notice. She had been having some radical thoughts concerning May and Mr Harvey. These came to fruition one quiet afternoon. Normally the doors were kept locked, just in case one of the patients decided to do a runner – old Mr Brown was once found in only his pyjama top wandering round Tesco.

Lucy saw that the key was in the door when she went to see Mr Harvey and May one day. Her impulses got the better of her and it was no time before she was ushering them through the door and out of the emergency exit at the back of the building towards her rusting little blue car. May and Mr Harvey needed no prompting. Laughing like children they creaked along, hardly escaping, but more tottering, they managed to get into the car. Mr Harvey was a little worried with the laughing, he knew what could happen but luckily Lucy had no idea. He pulled an old blanket lying in the back of the car under his bum just in case. May was thrilled to be out in the real world and stared out of the windows.

At the park Lucy prised them out of the car, wondering if she had done the right thing. Their reactions were more than she had hoped for. Mr Harvey went straight to the bench and as May and he sat down it was if they had found the Holy Grail. Their lined faces were illuminated and May touched the leaves and damp wood with her twisted hand; the day was warm and they lifted their faces up to the blue sky soaking in the colour.

Eventually May got them back to her car, and started on the journey home, in some apprehension. Lucy was getting worried. She knew she had done something very wrong and when she realised the car was low on fuel her agitation levels grew. As the little car drew into the petrol station her stress levels became so high she clutched her chest and fell onto the steering wheel in an eerie silence. May and Mr Harvey stared waiting for instructions and then finally Mr Harvey said, "I think she's dead." They were quite used to people dying around them, sometimes people slumped into the final sleep as Richard and Judy were doing their quiz, or once even disturbing the six o'clock news.

Poor Lucy had indeed finally burst her tender heart. The two old people sat in the petrol station.

"Have you any money?" May asked.

"No, but she does in her handbag," he replied.

They got her handbag out from under the seat and took out a £5 note. "This should be enough to get home."

"OK," agreed May. Opening the doors they squeezed out, leaving the car and Lucy abandoned in front of the pump. Out on the busy street there was a taxi rank. Mr Harvey tapped on the window of the first car, "£5 to see me and this good lady to the Sunset Retirement Home."

"OK mate, hop in."

The taxi dropped them at the back entrance and slowly, now very tired, they went round through the rhododendrons and looked at the windows. The door was firmly locked but one low-level window was open. A ladder lay against the building where a window cleaner had been working.

"Can you?"

"Can *you*?" she retorted.

Ten minutes later Nasty Nerys was shouting:

"Mr Harvey, why didn't you ask to go to the toilet!" May wished they would be quiet, she was missing Richard and Judy.

S. E. Coldwell, Sheffield

## Above and Beyond the Call of Duty

Brabham wearily stepped out onto the forecourt of Devonshire Road petrol station, the caustic odour of petrol fumes instantly invading his nostrils. A solitary blue Nova stood forlornly at pump number five waiting to be towed. Other cars had been kept at bay by the thin strip of blue police tape which flapped gently in the breeze as Brabham ducked underneath. The Nova's owner was laid out in the police mortuary along with the attendant who had the misfortune to be working that morning and based on the evidence so far it was going to be a long investigation. It wasn't so much that there was nothing to go on; hundreds of motorists used the petrol station every day and it was awash with traces of them all.

As the sun began to sink Brabham decided to take a walk in the small park across the street. It had been a nice day by all accounts, not that Brabham had seen much of it. On returning to his office an infinitely huge pile of paperwork awaited him, but he did not want to think about that right now.

The park was one of an ever-decreasing number of green spaces in the city that had not yet succumbed to the demand for housing developments. It was nothing out of the ordinary: a few scattered trees, clumps of bushes, grassy expanses, sparsely planted overgrown flower beds, litter, fly tipping, used condoms and the occasional hypodermic carelessly discarded. It was everything you would expect from an inner city park.

Brabham walked aimlessly for a few minutes before

coming across a park bench where an old man was seated, idly watching a Yorkshire terrier gambol through the long grass. When he looked up the man's face seemed strangely familiar but Brabham could not place him. Brabham sat down beside the old man and for a while they simply enjoyed the peace, and soaked up the dying rays.

"Tough day son?" the old man asked.

"You could say that." The peaceful silence was now broken and an awkward one ensued. This time it was Brabham's turn to break it.

"Do you come here often?" it was all he could think of to ask but the moment it left his lips he realised it sounded more like a corny chat-up line than a conversation opener.

"I come here all the time," the old man replied, not noticing Brabham's faux pas and added, "I like it here."

*Really?* Thought Brabham. What was there to like? It was tolerable enough now but it had no outstanding features. He had certainly been to better parks locally.

"I was here this morning," the old man went on.

What did that mean? Was the old man trying to tell him something? Brabham sat up a little straighter now but the old man did not elaborate.

"There was an incident over at the petrol station this morning, did you see something?"

There was that silence again. If the old man knew something he seemed to be enjoying giving it up, but eventually he spoke up again.

"6.14. It was just getting light. A young man, early twenties, wearing blue jeans and a grey sweat top came running across the field over there." The old man pointed towards a large sycamore tree. "He tripped by the tree and it looked like he had lost something but he didn't look very hard, just carried on running."

Brabham left the old man on the bench and went to investigate. This could be a promising lead: an eyewitness, and a youth seen fleeing the scene, but what could he have dropped? A murder weapon would be handy.

Brabham kicked around in the grass and soon found what he was be looking for. The old man was right, the kid couldn't have looked very hard – he must have been in a real hurry. But it was not a weapon. It was a key.

He donned a latex glove and retrieved the key from the grass, turning back to the old man; but the bench was empty and the park deserted. Even the dog had disappeared.

Brabham cursed himself. A possible eyewitness vanished and all he was left with was a key. He hadn't even got the old man's name. Why hadn't he told the old man to wait? Now he had nothing.

Back at the station Brabham reluctantly submitted the key as evidence. Forensics asked how he had found it. Brabham simply put it down to an anonymous tip which wasn't far from the truth.

But the key actually proved key to the investigation. Within a few hours Brabham received a call in his office. Forensics had managed to lift a finger print from the key which had soon yielded a name. A search of the database uncovered charges for petty theft, and drugs. In interviews with the attendant's co-workers, the same name came up as someone she had been out with a couple of times but it had not worked out: she hadn't said why, but her co-workers had never warmed to him the way she had. It was enough for Brabham to get a warrant.

At the house there was no answer. Round the side a ladder led to an open window, wide enough for a person who had lost his key to slip through. Armed response went in first as a precaution but they needn't have worried; when they found their man he was laid out on a bare mattress in a drug-induced stupor. An ambulance was called. While he was being taken away Brabham and his men searched the house. Brabham soon found what he was looking for. At the bottom of the wash basket was a bloodied grey sweat top, and wrapped inside that, the elusive murder weapon. Brabham was confident he could secure a conviction now, thanks to the old man.

He would have got here eventually, but not before the kid would have had time to pull himself out of it and get rid of the evidence. He just wished he could thank the old man for showing him the way.

On his return to the station, as he passed through reception, Brabham noticed an old black and white photograph mounted on the wall. Two men stood against an old oak-panelled wall, smiling out at him from beneath an emergency exit sign. The men were shaking hands; one held up an award for the camera. Brabham knew the old man's face had been familiar, though he was much younger in this photograph.

Brabham called over to the desk clerk, "Who is this in the photograph?"

The desk sergeant told him the name but it meant nothing to Brabham.

"What was the award for?"

"Longest serving community bobby – set some kind of record I believe sir."

"Do you know where he lives now?"

"Now, Sir?" The desk sergeant sounded puzzled. "Broughton Cemetery Sir, he died 15 years ago."

Joanna Styles, Malaga, Spain

## Escapology

"I'll lock you in while I fill up. Just in case."

When the four doors clunk shut around him, it's a red rag to a bull. Another opportunity to escape. Sean looks furtively round the inside of the Golf for the unlock button. There it is under the handbrake. Better wait till Mum goes in to pay. Another clunk as Mum puts the nozzle back and away she goes. Sean takes a deep breath – Houdini always had a calm, clear mind before an escape – and snaps on the handcuffs.

It's difficult to claw the seat belt off, and the handcuffs bite into his wrists, but one satisfying press later the doors unlock and Sean's on his way to freedom. Mrs Parker will be wondering where he is as she sits quietly on her bench, her back caressing the *'In Loving Memory of Stanley Parker 1921-2004'*. Sean's late for their meeting already, but Mum insisted he helped her at Tesco's with the Christmas shopping. Mark is at yet another football match and Dad's decorating the spare room for Auntie Jane's visit.

"Mrs Parker's always there anyway, Sean. It won't hurt if you're a bit late and I could really do with some help. I'll drop you off at the park on the way back."

But Mum doesn't understand about Mrs Parker. Mum doesn't understand about lots of things, but most of all about Sean's obsession with escape. For as long as he can remember, Sean has always wanted to escape. There's never a real escape plan because there's never really anywhere to go, but Sean relishes the challenge of getting out and away.

Mrs Parker understands this. Her Stanley always liked to get away – Blackpool was one of his favourites. And now that he has gone forever, there's nothing she wants more than to escape from life to join him. She tells Sean this every Saturday when they have what she calls her only proper conversation all week. "It's so lonely without my Stanley, you see."

And Mrs Parker's dad saw Houdini.

Sean sidles round the car towards the side of the petrol station looking for a way out. Exiting via the forecourt is too easy and obvious. Better if Mum can't see him. He's disappointed to find the wooden emergency exit gate unlocked – locked barriers are much more challenging – but he pushes through and ten minutes later, after running hard and fast, reaches the park. The December chill means it's quiet at this time, but Mrs Parker is there. She looks tired and somehow older than last week.

"Hello, Sean," she says, patting the bench beside her. "Stanley's been keeping this side warm for you. How did Houdini get here today?"

"Down a ladder," Sean's voice bursts with pride, "and out of a locked car. All with the handcuffs on!"

"Goodness me. You should be careful you know, you could easily fall." But in spite of her admonition, Sean can see she's impressed. Mrs Parker pulls out the handcuff key from her handbag and releases the cuffs from Sean's wrists.

The bit about the ladder isn't quite true. Sean was in his bedroom rereading the Houdini book Mrs Parker had lent him when a face appeared at the window, grinned and then disappeared behind a grubby cloth. Looking out, Sean could see the window cleaner's long ladder. An ideal escape route. Even more difficult with handcuffs. It was too early to go to the park – he always met Mrs Parker at noon sharp – but it was a tempting way to get out of his room and he wouldn't have to go to Tesco's. Sean jerked open the bottom window sash and for a brief moment enjoyed the vision of himself scaling agilely down.

"Sean, darling, are you ready?" Mum appeared at the doorway, her eyes registering the open window and the ladder. "Don't even think of it, young man. And you're not taking those handcuffs to Tesco's. I don't want people getting the wrong idea."

But Mrs Parker seems to believe all Sean's escape stories. She knows they are possible because her dad saw the real thing. The day Sean met Mrs Parker he was wriggling through the plastic play tunnel for the tenth time – on his front with his hands clasped tightly in the small of his back – when his eye was drawn to a glint in the sun on the tarmac path. He was disappointed to find the key wasn't treasure, but he liked the feel of the cold weight in his hand and spent a few happy moments wondering what it opened. A safe. A cage. Maybe even the Chinese Water Torture Cell. Then he noticed Mrs Parker, hunched on the lonely bench and guessed it was her door key. She offered him a grateful Extra Strong.

"You're getting quicker through that tunnel, young man. You must be pleased with your latest time, looked like ten seconds to me."

Flushed with pleasure, Sean told her about his eight seconds best time for getting out from under his bed with his feet tied and hands behind his back. And the handcuffs from the joke shop. And how he always had to get out of something. Then she told him her father's story about Houdini's Giant Milk Churn act in London.

"No one thought he'd ever get out. And when he did, nobody clapped at first. Stunned into silence they were. But then the crowd roared." She found the book in a trunk in her garage and lent it to Sean. "Don't get any silly ideas, now. This is just to look at."

She looked doubtful when Sean gave her the only

key to the handcuffs, but she could see the challenge and jumped at the chance of meeting every Saturday at noon so she could unlock them. "Promise not to put them on in the week. Just imagine what a fuss your parents would make."

But today, instead of putting the handcuff key carefully back into her handbag as she usually does, Mrs Parker hands it to Sean.

"I think it's better you have this now because it's my turn to escape next."

Sean's about to protest, but something in Mrs Parker's expression stops him. "And you keep that Houdini book. As a gift from me and Stanley."

As he watches her hobble down the path, Sean feels the handcuffs and their key grow heavier in his palm and he knows the bench will be empty next Saturday.

Swapna Dutta, Bangalore, India

## The Key

I'd never have climbed up the rickety ladder by the emergency exit of the dilapidated building if it hadn't been for the photography contest. It said 'unusual angles.' I imagined I might get something if I took the trouble to climb up and look around. But I never expected my zoom lens to focus on a lonely figure in the next building.

She lay on the bare floor, her clothes, books, and CDs scattered all over, looking the picture of despair. The room was not visible from downstairs. I would never have seen her had I not leaned out from the top of the ladder. Had someone locked her in? If so, why on earth didn't she scream for help? Surely someone would have heard her and come to her rescue by now? Or was she hiding from somebody? I just had to find out!

I looked around me. There didn't seem to be a soul nearby. I took a pebble from my pocket (I usually carry some when I go shooting) and aimed it at her window. She looked up, startled.

"Hi," I said.

"Who is it?" she whispered, peeping out.

"I've been taking shots of the building and just spotted you," I said. "Are you locked in by any chance?"

"I am but I daren't shout. He might hear me and bundle me off somewhere else," she said looking about her with frightened eyes.

"Look here, should I tell the police?"

"No, no, please don't!" There was real panic in her voice. "They'll never believe you. He has taken the key, you see."

"What key?"

"The key to my door, of course!"

"But the police will break it open, silly!" I assured her.

"DON'T tell them. It won't help matters," she insisted.

I didn't know what to think.

"I must speak to you," I said.

"Then come to my building – it's back-to-back with the petrol station – and come up to the top floor until you come to a locked door," she said. "But look out for a blue car at the petrol station when you pass it. It could be *him*. Wait until he's left."

I felt intrigued and darn sorry for the girl. It's not often one gets the chance to rescue a damsel in distress and this could well be just the scoop I'd been looking for. Far better than winning a photography contest in a newspaper! Strangely enough, the said blue car was there and I didn't particularly care for the scowling owner if this was the man the girl had been speaking of. But there could be scores of blue cars passing by without being related to her. Anyway, I made for the park in front of the building and sat on the empty bench, waiting for him to leave.

In a few moments I was rushing up the grimy staircase of the seemingly deserted building until I reached her locked door. I tapped gently.

"So you're really there?" her voice sounded excited.

"Now tell me, why don't you want to escape if you're really locked in?"

"Who says I don't? I just said, don't call the cops."

"Why?"

"Because they'll merely send me back to *him* again! It's happened before. They're all on *his* side."

"That's ridiculous!"

"Have it your way. I can't force you to believe me. But don't call the cops or anybody."

"Then how do you propose to escape?" I asked, puzzled.

"You've got to get hold of the key."

"By tracing the man in the blue car? Do you take me for Hercule Poirot or something?"

"No, just a man with some intelligence," she said. "He comes here every day to see if I'm OK. You could think up a way to get hold of it. Then I could escape quietly and no one would be any the wiser. But don't mention it to a soul. Promise?"

"Done!" I said.

It was an absurd situation! One that made no sense. People didn't keep captives like this. And yet this girl was locked in, sure enough! Who was the mysterious 'he' in the blue car? I decided to find out more before I did anything. I was outside her door once again the next morning. There was no sign of the blue car or its owner.

"Why has he locked you in?" I asked.

"Because I saw him kill her."

"Kill who?"

"My mother."

"Good heavens! Surely you can't be serious? People don't get away with that sort of thing these days."

"But he has. Because he is a doctor and everyone believes him."

"But why did he kill her?"

"To get hold of her money, of course! Isn't that obvious? You *are* dumb!"

"Who is he anyway?"

"My stepfather. He plans to keep me locked up until he can arrange to have me sent abroad. Then he'll dump me in a convent or something and everyone will forget about me."

"Don't worry, I'll do something!" I assured her. "What's your name, by the way?"

"Cindy. And yours?"

"Folks call me Sammy," I said. "Take care. I'll have you out soon."

I just couldn't imagine what I should do to set her free! Should I confront the man in the blue car and tell him I knew what he was up to? And that I'd fetch the cops unless he released her? Should I go to the police station first and tell them what I already knew? But could I be sure that the girl was speaking the truth? There was no doubt about her being locked in, of course. It seemed too complicated for me to tackle single-handed.

As I walked down the steps I saw the man in question coming up, a large key in his hand. I stopped. No time like the present, I told myself. Besides, he looked frail from close quarters and walked with a limp. I was more than a match for him, strength-wise. I could shove him down the stairs effortlessly.

"Just a minute," I said to him. "Give me your key."

The man started. "Did you speak to me?"

"You heard: give me the key!" I said. "I know you've got her locked up. You've no right – as you must know!"

"Who says I haven't?" the question fairly shot out.

"You're only her stepfather and—"

"Is that what Cindy told you?"

"That's not important. You've no right to keep her locked in a deserted building—"

"One moment, young man. Who says the building is deserted? Her room is part of my own apartment. If I've kept her locked it's because she needs it."

"Why?"

"Because I am her father and also her doctor," he said. "One has to be careful with schizophrenia."

"Schizophrenia?" I asked, bewildered.

"Yes, it's been really bad since my wife died of a sudden heart attack. Cindy came from school and found her. She imagines I killed her, that I'm not really her father—"

"Why don't you get her treated?" I interrupted.

"I am taking her to a special hospital next week. She is all I have."

His voice broke as he turned his face.

"Want to meet Cindy?"

And he handed me the key.

Halla Williams, Nailsea

## Cold

The park bench was crusted with rime but Corinne just *had* to put her shopping bags down on the way to the car, and the slush underfoot would be unforgiving to the insanely expensive Christmas presents she had bought Rob.

Gathering her chic, black suede coat under her bottom to insulate her, Corinne sat on the crunchy bench to rifle through the presents, worriedly checking that the Ted Baker shirt was not being crushed under the executive toy Rob would love. She panicked momentarily as she searched for the really important gift: the least expensive (but the most meaningful) was small and ordinary-looking, although she had added a presentation box and a flashy fob – the key to her flat. Thankfully, it was nestled at the bottom of the Gadget Shop bag, next to its much bulkier and more expensive competitor. What would she do if he preferred the toy? She tucked the precious little box into her coat pocket and leaned back on the bench for a moment.

The anxiety of the upcoming season of joy was getting to her; a tear of frustration leaked out from behind closed lids as she mentally shrieked '*When* will he ask me to the party?'

Rob was a typical man, Corinne noted. He looked at you askance if you exhibited the slightest bit of interest in what might be going to happen at the weekend, let alone two weeks from now. Corinne ran her finger carefully under each eye to check for runaway mascara, collected the handles of the bags together and stood awkwardly, wincing when the shopping banged heavily against her frozen, sheerly-stockinged legs.

Her long lunch had turned into the best part of the afternoon but Rob, who was her line manager, was out on a training course and no one at the office would tell on lovely, ditzy Corinne. Nevertheless, pulling out of the car park, she gnashed her teeth as she glanced at the petrol gauge and saw it was scraping empty.

The petrol station on London Road was crammed with cars behaving like dogs sniffing each other's backsides and growling threateningly from the edge of the pack. Corinne would never beep someone out of anger but the tears of frustration were creeping back, so she almost missed Rob's long-legged stride as he loped across the forecourt, back to an unfamiliar silver convertible with the stunning blonde from the adjacent office at the wheel. Corinne tucked wayward chestnut wisps behind her own ears in an unconscious attempt to compete as Rob leaned over to pull out and fasten the blonde's seatbelt for her. And then horror began to replace astonishment in Corinne's grey eyes, as the blonde took this opportunity to grab a confident and passionate kiss from Corinne's supposed boyfriend, before being honked off the premises by queuing cars.

Corinne would have to trust to the emergency reserve in her tank if she wanted to follow them, and she would also have to move faster than she had in her life. No time for tears now. Corinne hissed a breath out and wrenched the wheel into full left lock, bursting out of the queue and over the pavement, sending presents cascading off the back seat.

The Marriott Royal was where the course was being held, although it would be in full swing right now, so she was surprised when they descended into the car park below the hotel. She would be forced to abandon her own car in the lay-by to avoid being caught in the rear-view mirror.

Corinne did this without a second thought and strode into the hotel. Avoiding the concierge's attentive look, she marched to the lift that would go down to the car park. Turning aside at the last minute, Corinne took the stairs – she didn't wish to be facing them as they came up from the car park if they'd moved faster than she thought.

She needn't have worried; as soon as she stepped onto the parking level, she could see the convertible and the canoodling couple; she ducked behind the black Beamer next to her just in time: blondie pulled back from Rob's eager kisses and opened the car door. Wriggling out of his clutches, she offered him her car keys.

"I'm in room 201. Follow me up in five minutes and I'll be *ready* for you."

Rob's grin was lecherous and he took the keys, lounging back on the passenger seat and glancing at his watch before watching the strumpet wiggle off to the lift. Closing his eyes, he clearly enjoyed the next few minutes fantasising as Corinne's blood first boiled and then turned to ice.

Corinne got the key out of her pocket and out of its presentation box. She was about to toss it down the drain when a better use occurred to her. Watching Rob cross to the lift feet from her, she was tempted to reach out and stab him with it, but she had more than one target in mind for revenge. She let him take the lift and walked purposefully over to the smug-looking Toyota convertible. Keying a passable heart-shape on the bonnet, Corinne took a few moments to scrawl 'love Rob' down both sides.

Satisfied with the trouble that would cause, Corinne hurtled out of the car park through the emergency exit and into a plan that would ensure she was escaping that cheat for good. She raced up to her car and drove to a payphone to inform Head Office that Robert Waite's mother had been taken seriously ill and he should contact the hospital urgently. She imagined the reaction when he was found to be skiving from the training, the more so later when she wrote a grievance about how he had denied *her* requests for training and was keeping her subordinate to him because of their relationship (which he had pressured her into, of course).

Pausing only for petrol, Corinne hurried back to work and, once she had let herself be seen around the place, ducked into the ladies and, dropping her ditzy smile, examined her own face carefully in the mirror. Her eyes looked like arctic ice, her mouth curled at the corner with pleasure at her calculated revenge. She hadn't realised how little it would need to change her into the kind of woman who could knock someone off the corporate ladder and no doubt even climb it rapidly herself. She felt empowered, like there was nothing she couldn't do.

Stalking out of work at the end of the day, Corinne wondered how her revenge had played out. She pictured the row at the car, Rob checking his answerphone to find messages from Head Office, and the grievance being read with great concern in the Human Resources department.

Corinne closed her eyes on tears, of jubilation this time…

… and failed to see the convertible of a very upset blonde driver take the corner too fast and skid on the ice. The impact left Corinne's battered body lying in the slush with a frozen grin on her greying face.

"She was always smiling," wept her distraught mother at the eulogy. "Such a warm-hearted girl."

A.J. LeFlahec, Chambéry, France

## See no, hear no, fear no evil

*"No... more."* The old chimp signed. *"Kiki... too... tired..."* She slumped down, her chin sinking into her sagging chest and the wires of the electrodes falling in front of her face like a curtain of beaded braids.

In the cage next to hers, Falun flung himself against the bars of his prison, a wretched shriek filling the fetid air as he signed back. *"No take up! No take up! No take up!"* He raised his fist in the air, open/closed, open/closed, as though he couldn't stop himself. When Kiki, his surrogate mother, gave no response, he grabbed hold of the cold metal grille and set to shaking it with the strength of his youth.

A low rumble rose from the cage at the far end of the lab, silencing Falun and drawing Kiki's attention at once. Irving, the reigning gorilla, turned the hand resting on the ground sideways and lifted it slightly, palm up, while the other did the explaining: *"Give it a rest, Falun."* It's not *"No take up"*. It's *"No give up"*.

Falun gave a subtle nod before turning away, embarrassed. He'd only just begun learning human sign language. *"Kiki sad. Kiki sick. Sick/sad. Kiki stop soon. No stop Kiki!"* He dropped his hands to the ground and looked at Irving for understanding. On their own the signs meant so little, but his despair was evident even to the hardened gorilla.

Irving lowered his eyes and began signing to himself. *"What can Irving do? What can Irving do?"* Being the biggest primate in the lab gave him stature, but little more. He cast a wistful look in the bonobo's direction. If only he still had the youngster's vigour and enthusiasm, he'd be able to find a way to help Kiki.

But where would that get her? Her days were numbered. Besides, what better fate could any of them hope for? Twenty-odd primates in a run-down lab that reeked to high heaven of their own urine and faeces, mingling with fumes from the petrol station below.

Kiki might be the lucky one.

Irving's onyx eyes drifted away from Falun's cage to the wall behind it, where all the keys to the cages were lined up, labelled. Irving's eyes fell on the one that would have unlocked old Alpha's, if Falun's predecessor had not been a diminutive macaque.

Irving rubbed his scraggly chin and scratched his testicles absentmindedly. He hadn't given a thought to the keys in ages, not since Falun's predecessor had succumbed to the after-effects of an ill-considered experiment and Falun had been brought in as a replacement. A much *taller* one.

The gorilla let out a deep grunt, banging his chest for good measure. The permanent ruckus that reigned in the lab died down instantly as the other apes turned to look. At least he still commanded their respect.

Now, if only he could orchestrate their cooperation, something might come of it.

He pointed to Falun. Then he pointed to where the key hung. "*Get that thing.*" As though he'd been reading Irving's thoughts, the bonobo sprang into action and his arm shot out quick as a lizard's tongue. Falun strained painfully for as long as he could manage before letting his arm drop with a whimper.

Irving pointed to his toes. "*Use FEET!*"

Bravely Falun tried standing on the tips of his toes until he collapsed from the pain of it. Irving shook his head before he raised his own leg to show what he had meant.

Within a matter of seconds Falun gave a triumphant yelp. Dangling Alpha's keys in the air he gave in to the urge to hop up and down gleefully. All the others chimed in and Irving had no choice but to utter a roar so loud it shook even him.

"*Now pass the keys to Fritzie.*" The bonobo hesitated before handing them across the aisle to the tetchy guenon. Fritzie grabbed them and gave them a half-hearted shake before he too passed them on.

Would instructions be necessary every step of the way? Fortunately, an unexplainable sense of common purpose took hold of the otherwise uncooperative apes, and before Irving had time to sign directions, old Alpha was fumbling with the lock to his cage. As though he'd been doing it every day of his life, he turned the key and his door swung open noiselessly.

"*Get the OTHER keys, Alpha, one at a time.*" The old chimpanzee lowered himself to the floor and made his dignified way on all fours down the central aisle. He would show them that even at his age, a male of his stature was not to be dismissed. With grave deliberation he opened up the rhesus' cage before returning the key to its place on the rack. From there he directed the opening of all the other cells, one by one.

With all the cages unlocked, a single key lay untouched: the key to the emergency exit. As soon as that was opened, the alarm would sound. Even if they managed to unhinge the fire escape ladder, how far would they get before the firefighters arrived and started rounding them up?

The freed primates gathered by the exit, jostling for fearful peeks outside. Alpha set the tone for the exodus by placing a decisive foot onto the first rung and maintaining an even pace all the way down. The others followed – calmly at first, before the lot of them scrambled to freedom, swinging and jumping, some of them leaping as much as ten yards to the ground.

Falun and Irving stayed behind, waiting until the

other apes had reached safety. The gorilla then watched from a discreet distance while Falun gently plucked the electrodes off his beloved Kiki's shaved forehead. He helped her up and she attempted to exit the cage that had held her for fourteen years. But her frail limbs would not even carry her past the threshold and Falun was just quick enough to prevent her from collapsing over it. His face showing nothing but tenderness, the bonobo gathered her up in his arms like so many stems of delicate blossoms and placed her on his back.

Followed closely by a helpless looking Irving, they made their way down the ladder and across the street to a graffiti-covered park bench where Falun laid his precious burden down, careful to leave one hand between Kiki's head and the rough wooden slats, using the other to smooth down the sparse fur on her cheek.

Barely concealed behind the unkempt city greenery, in between rows of trash cans or peeking timid heads around the corners of darkened alleys, Kiki's old cell mates signed their silent farewells. But when the sirens sounded, one after the other they disappeared into the urban jungle, leaving her to cast her hopeless gaze up to the pale grey sky above, her one and only taste of the limitless expanse.

Had Irving been successful in his attempt to pry Falun away from Kiki's lifeless form, they might have had at least a temporary taste of freedom. But the bonobo hadn't the will to try a different life without his cherished Kiki, and Irving harboured no illusions about his fate elsewhere.

Emilia Blain, Canterbury

## Locked in Silence

Frankie with his orange hair and pale freckled skin loves her, of that she is sure. His good-humoured disposition and unerring loyalty never fails. Even when she calls him an ugly Ginger and his eyes glass over with tears, he dismisses her cruelty with a nervous laugh; a soft, sad sound that only serves to make the other students jibe.

Despite her unrelenting mockery, he remains. Good-naturedly accepting the harshness of her words, conceding that his family life is claustrophobic, inflexible. He agrees his dull father, reliant on a job at a local petrol station, is of value only because he will, one day, supply necessary tools for the mission. Frankie's mother, a dour woman with dung-coloured eyes, need never know.

Kate derides Frankie's parents and the private mode of their existence behind crooked net curtains. She scoffs at their home, an unimaginative suburban box accessed via a misshapen path and framed by overfed leylandi. Delicate porcelain mugs, white with hand-painted red roses, are reserved for visitors.

But what exposes Frankie's usefulness to her and her reactionary friends is his room. Che Guevara peers at them from a darkened corner of the ten by twelve space. They are pleased to see Frankie has rebellion running through his veins. He denies it; smears over his father's tenuous links to Cuba.

Kate's home offers only reliable misery. Her mother's grey eyes are glazed over by a comfortable lifestyle and monotonous domesticity. Her father's habitually silent presence is confirmed only by his bald head, visible above a broadsheet. And the small town, a transparent reflection of childhood haunts, like an old scratched movie where everyone moves too fast.

One day, the insurgents climb unseen, one by one, to the top of the ladder and onto the flat roof of the university library. In the distance the city looks small, eternal fog rising from distant factories, polluting air with poison. In hushed tones, self-righteously they convince themselves of moral duty against corruption. And so it is that Kate's university days grow turbulent with anarchic possibilities.

Frankie begins to drink; cheap red wine, rough and unpalatable. A worried frown a constant across his pale brow. A chill envelops Kate as she watches this formerly placid man transform. Once a conscientious objector, now he takes up the cause, leads her fair-rebellion friends. He begins to unnerve her.

Kate espouses temporary bulimia, an attempt to mould her body. Or is it a cry for help, an admission of self-reproach? She sets out to distract Frankie, to change his mind; revolve him to his former self. But talk of revolution has whittled innocence from his eyes forever.

Frankie says the rich and famous are self-absorbed enemies. He says he will end the suffering of all animals, human and non-human, by virtuous rebellion. Kate says she is frightened, no longer wants him to be a hero.

"The future is dismal," says Frankie, "a narrowing passage in a dark abandoned labyrinth." Anger flushes his face, a rash of scarlet infecting his porcelain skin. "This isn't living. Humans are trapped in the mundane."

Kate says, "You used to say there was nothing we

could do."

He pulls away, turns on her, eyes flashing, double flares against a thunderous sky. "You forced me down that road; I disagreed with you, and with all your friends." Mindlessly, he shakes his head. "What was it you said? 'It was an inevitability I was too cowardly to face.' I was angry inside but knew your words would force me towards this action, to a place of no return."

Kate places a hand against her blushed cheek, skin warm and tingling as if he's smacked her. Softly, she says, "Please don't go ahead with this. I was wrong."

He laughs, stomps across the room and out of the door. As it slams she hears him say he's going to see his father, to acquire equipment.

After an hour's agitation, already jangled nerves tightening, Kate wraps up in a long black coat, pulls a multi-striped woollen hat over dishevelled curly hair.

Arriving at the park, she sits down on a bench. Watching the children swing back and forth, her eyes track shadows lengthening and shortening under an unseasonably bright January sun. She feels like climbing to the top of the slide, wants to recapture an innocent childhood. Lifting her eyes to a bright sky, she watches wisps of cloud, sifted flour against pale blue silk. Controlling tears she asks God for forgiveness for hurting Frankie; if God is there that is, and willing to forgive.

As grey swirling clouds swallow up the lightness of the day, momentarily she thinks a storm is brewing. Her eyes fix on adults who halt the motion of the swings, are pointing to the clouds, pulling children up and into their arms. Kate's eyes follow the trail of spinning grey back towards its source. She swallows hard, realises inevitability has touched down.

By the time she reaches the laboratory the front of the building is charred, windows bereft of glass. She hadn't been sure where he would strike first, realises she should have known. Frankie's greatest sympathy is for what he calls sacrificial victims. 'The creatures suffer,' he'd said, 'so the rich and famous can wear make-up or perfume without fear of irritating their cosmetically enhanced bodies.'

Kate approaches a fire officer, asks what happened. He shrugs, whites of his eyes distinct against smoke-blackened skin.

Rushing in through the emergency exit, doors now gaping wide, Kate feels a hand on her shoulder.

"No heroics, love." The same fire officer drags her back, his large hand cupped beneath her fragile upper arm. "No one in there and the animals are based in a separate building."

Before she can reply the building explodes, carrying Kate away.

Devastating burns spatter Kate's body, searing crepe-like red and white patches, achingly raw. At Frankie's trial she is an almost empty shell, propped up and graceless in a wheelchair, only vaguely aware of what is happening. People stroke her stubbled head, say it is out of character, Frankie is young and disillusioned.

His strong presence in front of her is a lucid sensation; his smell warm, aromatic. Desperately, she wants to touch his firm hands, run fingers through his gingered hair; disclose her love for him.

The trial passes. Frankie's prison, a hospital for the criminally insane; Kate's within a damaged body.

Concentrating on the silent darkness, she is sure he understands her remorse; forgives her as she forgives him.

Once, when all was well between friends, she had no fear of the dark, but in the void that is Kate's life there is only fear and darkness. Her hours fill with random flashbacks; memories outside the realms of her control.

Friends are all gone now, swept away into a safe

subconscious which no key can unlock. There they remain ever young with eyes still sparkling, words full of promises to return. Faces from an ephemeral past, precious images preserved behind unseeing eyes, filling blank spaces in her hollowed out existence.

Alone now, she is but a fragile moth beating frail wings against tranquillity, her whole universe cocooned within her heart.

Tracie Barnett, Castlerock, Northern Ireland

Echoes

"Damn Kids, no respect for anyone!" grumbled Mr Jenkins as he shuffled his way out of the mini-shop.

A lady held the door open. He looked at her briefly and grunted. She smiled pleasantly. She was tall with short dark hair and, despite the stifling summer heat, was wearing a cream woolly jumper, brown trousers and comfortable shoes.

"Pump number 5, please," she said to the cashier.

Jenny Adelina Marsella, her red hair and pale complexion reflecting none of her Italian heritage, tapped at the keys of the till. "Would you like anything else?" she asked.

"No thanks," she said cheerfully. "Just the fuel."

Jenny watched the woman climb into her little turquoise car and manoeuvre her way around the silver car to the exit, where she had to wait for Mr Jenkins to cross.

At lunchtime, Jenny went to the park and sat facing the duck pond. She breathed in the air and looked up into the trees and watched the sun playing peek-a-boo through their dancing leaves. It was late August and only a slight breeze stopped it being unbearably hot. Two toddlers stood throwing oversized chunks of bread at the ducks.

A young couple, holding hands, walked in front of her. He whispered something in the girl's ear and she threw back her auburn curls and laughed. Her swing dress was perfect for the day but Jenny couldn't quite believe that someone could bear to wear tights on a day as hot as this. Jenny scrunched up her nose, making her freckles wrinkle, and scrutinised the lines that ran in straight lines down the back of the girl's legs; Jenny could have sworn that one of the lines looked smudged.

As Jenny turned to throw an apple core into the bin, she heard the girl laugh again but couldn't see where she had gone. As she stood up, she saw something in the grass. It was an old brass key. She picked it up and dropped it into her trouser pocket and sauntered home.

That night, Jenny slept fitfully. In her dream she was feeling her way along a wall; it was hot and she couldn't breathe.

"Where's the door? I can't find the door – I can't breathe, please help me someone!" She could make out an Emergency Exit sign but her eyes hurt so much that she couldn't keep them open. The relief of finding the door was replaced immediately with panic. She couldn't open it.

"Please someone help me!" She began to bang on the door with her fists. She tried to shout but no words came out.

Jenny sat up in her bed, her eyes wide and her heart hammering in her chest. She had never felt so relieved to be awake.

By 7.30 am the next morning, feeling shattered, Jenny looked bleary-eyed over the forecourt of the petrol station, and slid her hands into her pockets. She had forgotten about the key and took it out and held it in her hand. She turned it over and studied it closely. There were no distinguishing marks: just a scratched and well worn brass key. She couldn't be sure how old it was.

She wrote a note on a piece of paper – Found one key, in Guterson Park. Ask at counter – she stuck it on the inside of the door and put the key back in her pocket.

Later, as she strolled through the park, Jenny saw the young man from yesterday sitting on the bench. She pushed her hair behind her ears and bit her lip. She wasn't sure what to do: his hands covered his face, it was obvious that he was upset.

"Hey old man, where's your shoes?" shouted a voice; Jenny turned to see two teenagers running off. When she turned back, her heart jumped – the young man had gone but there sat old Mr Jenkins in his socks. And he was crying. Jenny sat beside him and passed him a crumpled tissue.

He suddenly started to speak, "I should have stayed with her but we had to save the little girl. Half her house was gone and she was just hanging there screaming. I ran to get the ladder from Alfie's garage, it was his dad's pride and joy, an 'Alco-Light' brought from America, one of the last to be manufactured due to the shortage of aluminium for the war effort. Anyway, I was trying to run with it. Elizabeth tried to help but her shoe came off, so I yelled at her to go to Grove's Grange, where I worked. It had a good cellar and I thought she would be safe."

As Jenny listened, her face creased in concern.

"When we got the child down the bombs were still dropping. Then all went quiet until the siren rang the all clear. I ran to the Grange trailing the little girl behind me. It was burning." Mr Jenkins started crying softly again. "I couldn't find the cellar key; it had been in my pocket, I kept checking but it wasn't there. We broke the door down but it was too late. They said it was the smoke. My poor Elizabeth."

He opened his hand and looked at a small sepia picture. "It was taken the last day we were together." Jenny's head started to reel, she felt sick. The photograph was of the young couple she had seen the day before.

Mr Jenkins stood, touched the brass plaque on the bench, then walked away on socked feet.

*My precious Elizabeth taken 25<sup>th</sup> August 1940*

That night Jenny dreamt again, except this time she was the little girl watching the young man as he frantically searched his pockets.

"Is this what you're looking for?" she asked in a small voice.

He grabbed the key from her small dirty hand and ran down the cellar steps.

The next morning Mr Jenkins came into the shop. Jenny hardly recognised him; he was smiling.

"About that notice on your door – I think you can take it off now." Mr Jenkins held the brass key between his thumb and forefinger.

Jenny stuck her hand in her pocket but the key was gone.

"Well, best I get off, I don't want Elizabeth to burn my bacon." He gave her an affectionate wink.

Jenny was still baffled when she went for lunch. As she approached the bench, she saw the lady with comfortable shoes smiling at her.

"Hello," she said. "Its Jenny isn't it? Thanks for finding my key. Mr Jenkins gave it to me. It belongs to my grandfather. We were going to clear out the garage. Alfie and Wilfred are great friends, they built the garage together after the original one burnt down during the war. Did you know that they used an old cellar door that came from the pub that the petrol station is built on? There's not much in the garage, years of junk and an old ladder."

Jenny wasn't listening, she was looking at the small brass plaque.

*To Wilfred Jenkins*
*Who Saved Me 50 Years Ago*
*Adelina Marsella*
*25<sup>th</sup> August 1990*

Jenny became aware of a memory she could not previously recall. Her grandmother had nearly died during the war.

Jamie McGaw, York

## On the Run

My chest burned as I ran. My eyes were streaming tears as the frozen air bit at them. My bike had slid out from underneath me on the slickness of the icy road at the corner of Penrith Road. It always had been unreliable. I couldn't restart it so I'd taken to my feet. One knee had been skinned under my jeans and I could feel the blood seeping through the grazes and sticking my trousers to the wound. Normally I would have stopped and sat, peeled back the fabric and nursed it tenderly. I was never the macho type. No time now. I kept running. I had to. Think Bruce Willis. Think Arnie.

I cut down an alleyway that ran parallel to Anna's street. Her place was my best bet. I couldn't go home and besides, I couldn't run much further. My throat was aching and the cold was eating up my lungs like acrid smoke. When I was halfway down the alley I slowed and made sure that I was in the shadows. Leaning my back against the wall and resting on my knees, bent double, I stopped for a moment and caught my breath – what was left of it. Considering my options I came to the conclusion that there were only two. Firstly, I go to the front door, I use the copy of the key that Anna didn't know I had, and I get in the easy way. The problem was that the front of the building was very open and well-lit and the neighbours were very nosy and likely to report intruders. Ironically, that was why Anna had always felt safe there. Bully for her. The second option was to break in through the back. I was less likely to be seen but it felt wrong. Don't ask me why, but whatever the situation it just felt like a bad thing to smash a window and break in to my ex-girlfriend's home. I would use the key instead. That's more reasonable. Less like breaking in. Some call it socio-pathic behaviour. I like to think that I'm more balanced.

I pulled myself up and started off again cautiously down another icy alleyway that would lead me directly past Anna's building and out on to the main road right by the entrance. The less open ground I had to cover the better.

The alley was covered in bin bags and smelt a little like urine, but it was dark. That was good. At the end of the alley I took out the small golden key that the cutter had prepared for me just a day before Anna had taken the original off me. She could be a real bitch. I got it ready and, making sure there was no traffic or people around I walked in a swift, casual manner to the front entrance. The key opened this door and the one to her apartment. I pushed it into the lock. Whether it was badly cut or just the ice, my luck wasn't in. Not only was it stuck but it wouldn't even come out of the lock. My fingers were cold and I couldn't even grip it. Someone shouted from above. My heart jumped.

"Hey! I thought Anna told you never to come back! She's out anyway! Get lost!"

I held it together and shrugged. I knew she was out, she always was on weekends. Her mother, the old bat, was ill.

"Sorry, I didn't realise... Good night..." I said and retreated back into the alley leaving the key stuck in the lock. I hoped that Mr Jefferies upstairs would be content with that. He seemed to be.

I went a bit further down the alley, out of view from the road, and pulled myself up over the high garden wall to the back of Anna's block. It wasn't much to look at; overgrown, a smashed green house, bits of wood and broken plant pots littered about, but no one could see me because of the shadows from the wall and the height of the building. My immediate panic was fading now. I felt that I had a moderate hiding place, but indoors would be better. I assessed the back of the building. Anna's place was on the first floor with an emergency exit that led to the hall in between her flat on the left and the one across on the right. It had an iron balcony with a set of pull-down ladders leading to each of the three higher floors consecutively. I quietly made my way over the pottery-strewn garden and found that I could just about reach the bottom of the ladder if I stood on the green wheelie-bin that had been thankfully left at hand by the tenants – most of whom considered themselves too respectable to do such common work as putting the bins out. I pulled gently at the ladder but found it unwilling to budge, and so yanked it sharply. It creaked loudly and rust fell into my eyes but no one came out to investigate; they were all in their front rooms or asleep by now. The ladder moved down quite smoothly after that.

I knew at the top of the ladders that I would never get through the fire door – those things are built strong – but I didn't have my eye on that. Anna always left her kitchen window open for the cat and I could reach it from the fire escape if I stretched. I had never liked that cat, it was a biter. Hopefully it had been run over since I left.

As I pulled myself through the window and flopped over the sink onto the kitchen floor like a seal I decided that I liked the cat after all. I was in. I was safe for a day or two. I smiled and looked in the fridge. It was cold outside but I needed cold juice to quench my thirst. I would have had a beer but she didn't drink them and she wasn't buying them for me anymore.

I went through to the hall and smiled again: she still had it. I sat down on the garden bench that we always used to sit on when it was under a huge sycamore tree in the park. Anna used to say that we had all of our best times on that bench.

When she dumped me I nicked it and stuck it in her hallway in an attempt to get her back. She said I didn't get it and took away my key.

I didn't get it then. But I suddenly realised how self-obsessed I was being. What's more, she probably couldn't move the bench by herself. Maybe if I put it back in the park... Maybe that would make her happy.

There was a knock at the door.

It was the Police.

Open up.

They know I'm in here.

They know I robbed the petrol station.

I was seen on CCTV.

I was seen trying to force entry here.

Mr Jefferies had dobbed me in. He used to suspect me of everything... He was usually right.

Sharon Birch, Hartlepool

## A Kind Of Loving

I picked him up on a park bench and offered him a tissue with a sympathetic smile. He took both.

That was the beginning of our relationship and I always held the power in my tightly curled-up fist. Understanding and compassion made him come to me. After so many years, my craft had been practised and I was always good at spotting the vulnerable ones.

We met in secret for weeks until eventually he built up the confidence and took me home. It was his choice. I liked the ones from the well-off families best. They ignored their kids and gave them money and other things to keep them amused. With no personal time to give their children, the youngsters were receptive to me.

This one, Danny Young, unfortunately came from the scummy kind of background; the sort of family that didn't care where their kids were, just as long as they weren't hanging around the house making a nuisance. These families didn't have the cash to flash. It all went on fags, cheap beer and the odd bit of whizz. The posh ones called it neglect but they were equally as bad. They might have had fancy cars and big houses but they never gave the attention that the children craved or deserved.

This left the door nicely open for me.

Danny's mother was living with his father's brother and the door was open to other services too. His dad lived round the corner and came round everyday. Two of his oldest brothers were inside and his two youngest ones were heading that way. His sister was pregnant at fourteen and now, at twenty, had three kids. They lived in the next street. Danny often stayed with her until she found a smack-head boyfriend who beat the crap out of him. That's when I found him and I stepped in.

None of them cared about him but they liked me, didn't doubt me. I told them I'd been a youth worker in the town I'd previously lived in and they had no reason to disbelieve it. It was a sort of truth anyway. They liked my influence on Danny. He now had some manners and I taught him that it was best to help out at home and no one would be on his back if he behaved himself. It worked and they didn't bother about me taking him out here and there. They liked it, especially when I hired a minibus and took them all out for the day. It nearly killed me to do it, but it was worth it. A trusted friend, I became. I took Danny places his family couldn't, bought him things his family wouldn't. He was out of their way; they liked me, trusted me and even encouraged me.

A kind of grooming the officials call it, manipulation. For me, it's the key and it works.

I'd slip him a fiver now and again and Danny was grateful. I bought him a new pair of trainers, the kind he'd never had. When he had a school photo taken and wanted to ditch it because no one would want it anyway, I put one on my car dashboard. He saw it on my computer desktop too, when he came to visit for the first time. He blushed and thanked me.

It was easy after that. He was all mine.

I suppose I became greedy, complacent. One night it was late and we'd been looking at porn on the computer. Between us, we had drunk a bottle of wine, more him than me, but I couldn't drive having had a drink. He wanted to stay the night so I let him. It was simple.

It was a step too far.

The next day, as I pulled into the petrol station for refuelling, a police car pulled up alongside us. It didn't bother me but Danny looked uneasy. I gave him the money and sent him in to pay. The female cop followed but only to buy a paper. Danny panicked and made a run for it through the emergency exit, out the back door and straight into a courtyard.

Of course, they were suspicious. He looked guilty of something and acted it. They checked him out, then me. I could tell she knew, that female cop. I saw her look at Danny's photo on my dash. She questioned me, eyes narrowed, distrustful. She asked if I loved him. Cheek! Of course, I did, but I wasn't going to give it away, that would be telling.

Sitting here now, in my cell, I have to admit that Danny was different. He was gentle and kind. Not rough like his undeserving family. I could have given him such a better life. If only it had been after his sixteenth birthday, they wouldn't have bothered checking me.

It's like climbing a ladder see, and I was almost on the top rung. I very nearly had him for good. One step at a time and gently does it. He'd have been mine forever. His family would have willingly given him up to live with me, come his birthday. It was one less for them to worry about.

They caught me the first time, teaching young boys to swim. I took them to the top and then they'd jump in from the highest rung. They look so god-damn handsome in their little swimming trunks, I couldn't help myself.

I learned to pick older targets after that and there were so many. After all, adolescent boys are so grateful for any outlet for their raging hormones.

And nobody suspects a middle aged female.

M. A. Rodger, Poole

## It Won't Go Unnoticed

Inspector Carver rather enjoyed his occasional forays out with the night patrol, his 'firsthand refreshers at the grassroots.' PC Dainty didn't. He just wished the Inspector would choose someone else to get *refreshed* with. Did he always have to pick on him?

"Pull in here, Dainty."

Dainty didn't need telling. Every time, halfway through the patrol, Inspector Carver made sure they visited this out-of-town petrol station at the crossroads. The toilet was the usual reason, sometimes even urgent enough for the blue flashing lights, although Carver was also attracted by the ample supply of discounted sandwiches always on offer late at night. It was a quiet night, thankfully – only one other vehicle on the forecourt as Inspector Carver sprinted across to the toilets beside the garage shop.

The first sign of something amiss was the garage cashier frantically waving at Dainty who secured the patrol car and entered the shop.

"Quick! A bloke's just ran off through the back, through the emergency exit. He hasn't paid."

Dainty's training told him not to go running out into the night after some unseen thief. He positioned himself so he could keep an eye on the exit, in the far corner of the shop beyond the racks of motor oil, tool kits and stepladders.

"What did he take?" He had visions of some twelve year old legging it across the fields with a ten-foot stepladder.

"A hundred and thirty-seven litres of diesel."

"What?"

"The white truck. He was the driver." The cashier waved an arm towards the unattended Y-reg truck parked beside the pumps.

"Technically that's not theft," Dainty explained, "not unless he drives away without paying." Somehow this didn't seem to calm the already frantic cashier. "Perhaps he got confused. Perhaps he was looking for your toilets."

"No way. He saw you drive up and, wham, he was gone."

Hearing this, Dainty took a quick look outside the emergency exit. Black as a coal hole. No chance of finding anyone out there who didn't want to be found.

"OK. I'll check if the vehicle's stolen." The cashier was greatly cheered hearing this but Dainty felt more needed to be said – to prevent problems later. "If it's not stolen, there's nothing we can do about it."

"But it's blocking up half my forecourt!"

"Let's just see if it's stolen first, shall we, sir?"

The Inspector reappeared as Dainty walked out onto the forecourt to make the call. He explained the situation then radioed in from the patrol car. The reply came back promptly – with the Inspector along replies always did. The truck was not reported stolen, news which momentarily dampened the Inspector's enthusiasm. He liked nothing better than *'putting the mockers on blaggers and villains'* – if only policing was that simple.

"If the truck's not stolen, what's the betting he's carrying a load of drugs. Or illicit booze. Or illegal immigrants," suggested the re-enthused Inspector.

The back of the truck was open but their view inside was blocked by its broad loading hoist folded up against the back of the truck.

"You'll need the keys to operate that." Dainty knew

about these things. His uncle was a lorry driver.

"Or you could just ask the cashier to lend us of one of those stepladders he sells," suggested the Inspector smugly.

The cashier proved happy to assist, even helping Dainty carry the ladder outside. Then the Inspector took charge and, armed with a flashlight from the patrol car, clambered up to look inside.

"Seats," he called down disappointedly. "A whole load of old park benches."

"Stolen, do you think, sir?" asked Dainty.

"Hardly likely. Far too many for thieves to have gathered together. You could kit out half the parks in the county with this load. And anyway, most look ready for the scrap yard."

"But what about my forecourt?" pleaded the cashier. "It's blocking half my pumps!"

Dainty drew the cashier away from the truck. "We can make an official report, sir, but without a crime having been committed or public safety being put in jeopardy, there is nothing more we can do."

"At least move it away from my pumps. See, there's a gradient. You only need to let the brakes off."

"And the steering lock, sir. You'd need to steer it and you can't steer without the keys."

"Come on," interjected the Inspector. "The constable will log the incident while I buy my sandwiches. And calm down. I'm sure a petrol station makes this a public safety issue."

That cheered up the cashier. It took Dainty some time helping return the ladder then logging the incident to ensure a tow truck would attend and Inspector Carver was in no hurry, engrossed in choosing his sandwiches. But all this was rudely interrupted by the sound of a seven-ton Y-reg Volvo truck starting up and rapidly driving off into the night.

Dainty, much practised in such emergencies, radioed

in the incident as he started the patrol car but the Inspector was in no hurry.

"What's the panic, constable?" he asked as he lumbered into the passenger seat loaded down with sandwiches, chocolate bars and crisps. "Where's he gonna go?" The lorry had turned towards town – no side turnings for over two miles.

Dainty sensed the Inspector was now revelling in this night patrol. Coming up with the right decisions – the ladder, calming the cashier, knowing not to rush – not the mark of your usual out-of-touch top-brass officer living in an ivory tower. Inspector Carver was bound to ensure this little incident at the petrol station didn't go unnoticed by the lads on the beat.

"Less haste, more speed," he declared, at last shutting the patrol car door.

As he spoke the radio called through.

"All units. A five-eleven, RAPF Ltd. Whitefields Industrial Park."

The Inspector grabbed the receiver. "Show us attending the five-eleven."

"What?" Dainty couldn't understand.

"Come on constable. Aggravated burglary has higher priority than a tank-full of stolen diesel."

"I don't think so sir. And Whitefields is twelve miles away. There'll be plenty of units nearer than us."

"It was an 'all units' call, constable. Remember your procedures."

"But—"

"Don't argue. Drive!" So they turned the car towards Whitefields and the white Volvo truck was allowed to escape unhindered.

But Dainty hadn't forgotten his procedures. The 'all units' message was for information – there was no instruction to attend. And five-eleven was 'aggravated burglary no longer in progress', a serious incident but lower priority than preventing the Volvo's escape.

However, Dainty had been expressly ordered not to argue. So he drove, obediently, blue lights flashing. It was no surprise to find that half the relief had arrived at Whitefields before them.

And the look on Inspector Carver's face told Dainty he wouldn't be taking the Inspector out on future night patrols – not for a very long time – if ever: the look on Carver's face as he caught sight of the burgled factory. *'RAPF Ltd – Renovators of Antique Park Furniture.'*

'Golly,' thought Dainty sardonically, 'our little incident at the petrol station certainly won't go unnoticed now.'

Helen Meikle, South West Rocks, NSW, Australia

Quirks of Fate

Joely liked park benches. If you got in early and picked right, you could quite often get one to yourself and spread your things out like it was your own private desk. He had his favourites, ones where there was plenty to see but still enough bushes so you could hide from nosy old cows wanting to know why you weren't at school. Not that he couldn't go to school if he wanted, it was just...

He shrugged, flicking the thought away like a persistent fly. Time to get moving, probably. *He* would be down the pub by now, and the convenience store next to the Underground would be busy enough so he could pick up something for tea.

But it was never that easy, was it, Joely thought bitterly. His ribs were hurting as he trudged up the stairs to the flat an hour later. His mum had been right. Walking under ladders sucked. The one they used to stack the shelves at the convenience store had been right in front of the beans, and he'd had to squeeze in to reach the ones he wanted. And then, just when he'd got his hands on them, some dumb copper had hit his siren right outside the door and scared the piss out of him so he'd jumped, and the ladder had come down with a mighty crash. But he'd got away, even though he'd tripped over the step and fallen flat on his face and the beans under his jacket had smashed into his ribs and he probably had a few broken ones at that. Like anyone cared...

Still, he had the beans, best brand and all. He could

feel his mouth watering as he reached the top landing and tiptoed across to listen at the door. Sure enough, there was no sound of his dad's heavy breathing or angry mumbling, and he reached for the string around his neck with a sigh of relief.

It wasn't there.

He dropped the stolen beans on the floor and pulled frantically at the front of his shirt. It *had* to be there! He remembered tying it on this morning. He *never* forgot his key! But it was gone. Instead, his scrabbling fingers found a line of chafed skin where the string had pulled hard before it broke. It must have happened when he fell, and now it was gone.

For a moment, he thought he might cry. He sat on the top step with the beans beside him and couldn't bear to think about it. What was he going to do?

Joely pulled himself together. He was ten, now. Double figures. He could look after himself – he had learned how to shoplift – and that meant finding his key.

He got slowly to his feet, looking around for somewhere to hide the beans until he got back. The landing didn't offer much, just bare walls and a thin, mucky carpet. He opened the door to the fire stairs and picked his way carefully down the concrete steps between the lumps of old rubbish. There was a pile of rubble at the bottom that would do nicely. He pushed the tin in behind a chunk of rock and let himself out the emergency exit. And that was when Fate stepped in.

There was a car in the lane between the flats and the petrol station in the next street. Its engine was idling, and just as the emergency exit shut behind him with a loud thud, two men in balaclavas came barrelling round the corner from the direction of the pumps. As the car revved and switched on its headlights Joely jumped for the shadows before he could be spotted.

But he crashed into the path of the smaller of the two men, who instinctively scooped him up as he threw himself headfirst onto the back seat of the car.

They took off with a screech of tyres. Joely was gasping for breath with the man almost on top of him, and struggled to sit upright as the car cornered fast into a maze of back streets.

"Bloody hell, that was close!" the driver shouted out, turning to glare over the back of the front seat. "We could have... shit, Matty, what's that?"

Joely's assailant looked around in confusion, as if a bomb might have sneaked into the car. "What's—?"

"The kid, Matty, what's the kid doing here?"

"Well I dunno... I mean he just—"

"The boss is going to kill you for this! You know the rules. No one gets hurt. And kidnapping... shit!"

"Hey, it wasn't like that! He just—"

"Shut up, will you!" the big man roared. "Just shut the hell up, I have to think!"

But whatever thoughts he had didn't include letting the kid go. Any other time Joely might have been pleased – he didn't get to ride in cars much – but as it was, sheer terror was only nudged aside by an almost overwhelming need to pee. So he had barely noticed his surroundings when a lift finally disgorged them at the door of a neat little flat; the battle triggered by his presence raged over his bent head until desperation forced him to look up. The sight that met his widening eyes was almost too much.

"A-Adam?" he stammered, just as the man in front of him said "Joely?" and they stared at each other in stunned silence.

"I need to pee," Joely managed at last, and without a word the man led him down a short hallway and into the coolest bathroom Joely had ever seen. By the time he emerged, everyone had gone except for his tall, elegant half-brother Adam, the hero of his babyhood and now clearly a person of substance – although the origins of that substance seemed dodgy to say the least.

"Joely! What were you doing there, for God's sake?"

Joely was under no illusions. Adam wasn't talking about his trip to the bathroom. He shrugged. "Lost my key, didn't I."

"So knock on the door. Where's your mum?"

Joely looked up, startled. "She died. Didn't you—"

But he didn't, of course. If he had, he'd have done something. They both knew what the old man was like. The knowledge sat there between them like a third presence.

"Shit, Joely!" For a moment Adam slumped, driving his hands through his dark hair as if to squeeze the implications of it into his skull. "I'm sorry." He straightened, squaring his shoulders and taking a deep breath. "Well, it's just us then, isn't it," he said, and held out his hand.

An hour later, Joely curled up between clean sheets in a room that smelled of fresh air instead of dirty socks and thought of his favourite park benches. He almost dared hope he would never see them again.

In the living room, Adam contemplated a future where robbing petrol stations no longer featured and little brothers did. It scared the shit out of him. But what could you do?

"And who knows?" he murmured. "It might be the making of us both."

Cally Taylor, Brighton

Sam the Scam

When Sam ran out of the petrol station, dripping with orange juice, we legged it down the High Street and into the park. That's where I am now, slumped on a bench, panting and sweating. I was sitting on this bench last week, playing a game on my new mobile, when Sam came over and bummed a fag off me. I don't normally get on with other kids, but Sam was different. He wasn't from my school and he was sharp.

"You're like Johnny Vegas," he said to me, "but not as funny."

"And you're a scammer," I said. "You've had four fags off me now."

Sam likes scamming. Now it's his name too – Sam the Scam. He christened himself ten minutes ago, with a carton of juice that he scammed from the petrol station and poured over his head.

Orange juice drips from his ears – they stick out a bit but I don't take the piss. I could, but I don't. He's my new best mate.

"So... tell all, Sam."

Sam tells the story, machine-gun fast.

"I said I was having a hypo and needed something sweet urgently. I rolled my eyes and clutched the counter and they fell for it. They got me a chair and gave me a carton of orange. I took a sip then poured the rest over my head and ran the hell out of there. You should have seen their faces, man."

Sam sticks his hand in the air and I high five him.

"Hey," he says after we've both stopped laughing.

"Want to get in on a new scam, Fatty?"

"What's that?"

"We nick dogs, hold them to ransom and make a bit of cash."

"How?"

Sam rummages around in his pocket.

"I've got that all figured out," he says, holding up a key. "See this? This is the key to our own little dog pound. Now let's go get us a dog."

The first dog Sam spots is a little West Highland Terrier, the kind posh people like. We don't even have to get up from the bench; it just wanders over when we call to it. Sam looks around to check no one's looking and then offers the dog a Mars Bar he nicked from the petrol station. The dog sniffs and inches closer. Sam grabs its collar and scoops it up into his arms.

"Run Fatty," he shouts. "Run!"

Sam sprints ahead and I run as fast as I can behind him. We weave out of the park gates, across the road and down a side street.

I start to feel like I'm going to puke when Sam finally stops running.

"Here," he says, pointing at a rusty old garage door.

"What?"

"Our dog pound," Sam grins. "Aka my brother Glynn's lock-up."

He fiddles the key in the lock until the handle finally turns, then yanks at the door. It slides up about a foot and then stops.

"It sticks," he says. "We'll have to squeeze under the gap."

"Are you kidding?"

The dog barks and Sam glances down the street.

"Shit," he says as he drops to the floor, holds the dog to his chest and scoots under the gap. "Suck it up, Fatty, someone's coming."

I squeeze my way through the gap and Sam pulls the door down after me. It clanks shut. It's pitch black inside so I spark up my lighter. The faint light reveals Sam's grinning face.

"Piece of piss," he says.

"So what now?" I ask. "How do we get the money?"

"Look at the dog's collar," he says. "There should be a little metal tag with a phone number and the dog's name on it."

I move the lighter closer to the dog's neck, being careful not to singe its fur.

"Sam, there's no tag."

"You're kidding?"

"Nope."

Sam starts feeling the collar, running his fingers all the way round the dog's neck.

"Shit!" he says. "Shit. Oh..."

His eyes don't look right and he's shaking. Even the little dog is jumping around in his arms.

"Sam what is it?"

"I'm having a hypo."

"Don't kid around, man."

"No, Fatty," Sam leans against a wall. "It's for real this time. I'm diabetic. I shouldn't have dropped that bloody Mars bar when I grabbed the dog."

I pull at the garage door. It's jammed shut.

"Shit," I say.

I shove my hand into my pocket and pull out my mobile phone. It's the best you can buy.

"I'll call 999," I say.

"No," Sam says. He puts the dog on the floor and sits down. "They'll take too long. I need something sweet now."

"But we're locked in..."

"My fault mate," he says, "Glynn told me it locks on the inside and I forgot."

He points about seven foot up the opposite wall,

"There's a window, Fatty." He squints into the darkness. "And a ladder. You'll have to climb out of the window."

"What? Shit. OK."

I drag the ladder up against the wall and I'm about to put my foot on the bottom rung when Sam shouts my name.

"Leave me your phone," he says. "Just in case."

I carefully throw the phone to Sam and start to climb the ladder. The window is a tight fit but I manage to squeeze through. I have to drop into a metal skip below which winds me, but I'm shitting myself so much about Sam that I hardly feel the pain. Before I know what I'm doing I'm sprinting back through the park and towards the petrol station. My chest aches and the sweat is pouring down my face as I run in. I grab a handful of Mars bars from the confectionary counter and speed back to the automatic doors. They slide shut.

"Stop!" shouts the guy behind the counter. "Shoplifter! Stay where you are."

I scan the shop, desperately looking for a way out. There's an emergency exit right next to the drinks cabinets so I speed towards it. I press down on the bars and barrel my way through. An alarm starts to wail but I keep running.

When I get back to the lock-up my sweatshirt is stuck to my back and my hair is plastered to my forehead. I clamber onto the skip and reach up to the window. I'm not strong enough. I can't pull myself up.

"Sam," I shout. "Sam, I've got some Mars bars. Are you OK?"

Inside the lock-up the dog barks.

"Sam!" I shout again. "Sam, can you talk?"

I jump off the skip and run round to the front of the garage. I yank on the handle and the door slides open a bit. As I squeeze my way through, the dog, barking

its head off, runs past me and onto the street. I let it
go.

"Sam," I call into the darkness. "Sam, are you OK?"

I spark my lighter and stare at the place where Sam
was sitting.

"Sam?"

I walk round the whole lock-up several times until
the wheel on the lighter starts to burn my thumb and I
let it go out.

Sam has gone. So has my phone.

Tracey Clues, Keighley

Tramps and Ladders

As he sat at the lights, tapping impatiently, the tramp walked past, waving his gratitude for those that had stopped. *At least he's got time to be civil.* It was late and Clifford was rushing to get home to Marlene before she threw his dinner in the bin. She wouldn't stand for it twice in one week: 'Lateness is the ultimate rudeness.' She said it with her headmistress hat on.

Today was Bingo and Ethel would already be there, revving up her Micra as if she were supplying background effects for Meat Loaf – Live on Tour. Clifford knew they wouldn't go until he got home; the spectacle of him cowering as Marlene propelled cold shepherd's pie at his head was too much gossip to miss.

*It's no good; I'll have to stop.* The red fuel light had been glaring at him for the past five miles and there was town traffic yet to go. Besides, he didn't fancy queuing early the next morning – Budget Day. The pumps would be drained; panic-buying before the guy with the red tin lunch box bumped the price up.

*Left side, left side.* He often forgot, pulling into the wrong lane, then wondering if he should wrestle with the pipe or admit defeat and drive round to another pump. Every other car he had driven was a driver-side-fill-up; this was alien green and alien-sided. Even the headlights were on the wrong side of the steering wheel.

The pump clicked, hostile to his impatience. Leaning

back on the trigger, he felt the liquid throb through to the tank. For a long moment he was mesmerised. Closing a deal, living a dream, escaping...

Another click. He paid for the petrol and a sandwich – he'd need some tea. *Better leave that in the car, though. She'll think I've been late on purpose.*

*No sign of Ethel's car – maybe she's cried off.* This was good, and bad. Marlene's audience was absent, but would bingo-withdrawal spark her fury even more? Clifford closed the door on the sandwich. He'd see how the land lay first.

The house was dark, apart from the security-activated lamp on the coffee table. *That timer needs changing – the church sets its clock by that lamp.* He fumbled in his pocket for his key, his woody fingers feeling for the cold, brass stem of his house key amongst the sticky wrappers and escapist pennies.

"Why aren't all your keys together?" It was only her nagging voice in his head, but he still turned back a little, expecting her to see her moaning behind him. She could never understand the weight wasn't good for the ignition. He pulled out his hand, flicking the waxy papers off his fingers and promptly dropped the whole bunch on the ground. In midsummer, this wouldn't have been a problem. Tonight, it was dark. As he pushed forward to crouch, his foot made the fatal error. He heard the sickening splash as his fingers reached, eternally hopeful, for the bars. Actually, a deep drop rather than a mere splash.

*Damn.* More ammunition for Marlene. She'd love this one. At least it'd cure her disappointment over the bingo. He gulped before knocking. Suddenly his own front door was the headmistress's office.

She didn't come. He knocked again. Still no answer. He didn't panic, but strained his ears for the east end twang on the television. No twang and still no footsteps.

Hmm. Either she was out, or she was in and ignoring him. Or just maybe there was something wrong. *What if...* No, that was ridiculous. *I need to get in.* He looked with a smile at the second bedroom window; his bedroom window. Open, as always, and right above the garage.

Jeff Jenkins' ladder was resting against their car port. Lightweight and portable. Easily borrowed, insufficiently secured, quickly climbed, gracelessly dismounted. Clifford's wrist groaned on its own behalf as it slapped the hedgehog boot-brush; Clifford's mouth was unable – his unconscious brain wasn't in a position to speak.

In fact bingo had been brought forward and they came home early. Ethel giggled all the way to the hospital; Marlene tutted. Clifford preferred the moments when his consciousness scuttled off, taking the tuts and giggles with it. And that hat – like a chimeric watermelon in leprechaun green. 'My lucky hat', she'd say. *Maybe you feel lucky...*

The sign fluttered into focus above his head, dipping beneath the watermelon's feathers. Emergency Exit. *Can I get one of those? An exit from this life.* But the beep was still strong – he wasn't getting out yet.

Ethel's voice filtered through the beeping. "How silly... climbing on the garage roof... should've used the door..." The high pitch insulted him, as did Marlene's eyes as she glared into his sockets, burning him.

"Why were you up there? What on earth possessed you?" Marlene could be so patronising.

*Should I tell her?* Mulling it over, he decided not to bother. The way her concrete face was setting, she didn't need much incentive to start lecturing. Losing his key down that drain so near the door was something she had been warning him not to do for years.

"How long do I have to stay in?" His blasé tone caused lip-curling on both women. *Damn, too cheerful.* "Or can I go home?" *Too predictable, too late.*

"The doctor says..." – it sounded like she was reading the news – "you might be able to come home tomorrow. I've got to look after you – apparently." She tried to sound annoyed, but her sadistic smile belied the suggestion. "Best be going now. Lots to do. You coming, Ethel?" No goodbye kiss; he should have known better.

Nothing comforted Clifford in his scratchy sleep. Thoughts intruded on his peace: being fussed over wasn't an option. Hell on earth, that was his predicament. Her looking after him all over again, just like the time he'd had mumps.

The park bench near the pond was beckoning, welcoming. Tramps didn't have suffocating step-mothers smothering the life out of them, did they? They could lie amongst the bushes and trees, calm amongst the green, living day to day. Could he get away with it? Or was he being naïve?

Sarah Ann Hall, Maidenhead

Escape Flight

The answerphone's insistent red light was blinking when Lucy got in from work. She pressed play.

"Hello, darlin'. I'm on leave, as it were. I'm coming visiting."

Lucy froze. Jimmy's frosty voice. Last known address care of Her Majesty. She'd moved since he'd gone in, twice. How had he got her number?

It didn't matter. She had to get away. If Jimmy was coming looking, she was going elsewhere.

She stood motionless in the dingy hallway. Any minute he might knock at the door, ring again to check whether or not she was home. She couldn't delay, had to go. Her keys were in her pocket. Did she have time to pack a bag? Wherever she was going it would be better to arrive with deodorant and toothbrush.

Five minutes later she was in the car with an overnight bag heading into town. She'd tell Melissa she was leaving. She still didn't know where she was going, maybe Melissa would have an idea. Being the older, prudent one, she might even be able to lend Lucy some money. The hole in the wall would only laugh as it swallowed her card however hard she pleaded with it to be helpful.

The journey towards town passed in a blur, her head buzzing with ideas and countermands. As she passed the parade of shops on the outskirts she looked over at the flat she'd shared with Jimmy. She recognised Dan, her old landlord, cleaning the windows. The ladder was perched precariously with no one to hold it steady. Jimmy and Dan had cleaned the windows together when they'd lived there. Jimmy taking his life in his hands up the ladder while Dan ostensibly held onto the bottom, chatting to any bit of skirt that happened to pass by.

She turned away from memories to check her rear view mirror. That grey car. It had been with her when she'd pulled out of her road. So what? No one would be following her. Paranoia forced her to drive around the block. The grey car went too.

Lucy scanned ahead as she drove. No police cars when you want one. She was too nervous to use her phone, and besides it was in her bag, safely out of reach on the back seat.

She ran the double set of traffic lights at the end of the high street. The grey car had no chance, stuck as it was behind a post van. If she caused an accident the police would be called and she'd be safe. As it was the delay on the lights ensured she was across and well out of sight before the traffic began to move.

She parked opposite the club where Melissa worked and ran across the road. Darkness blinded her momentarily before she found her bearings and went through to the bar where Melissa was carrying out a stocktake.

Lucy explained about the phone call, her need to get away, about being followed.

"Here, take the key for the emergency exit. You won't be seen. Just be careful crossing back over the road."

"It's an emergency exit with a key?" Lucy frowned.

"That's where the burglars were getting in, so it's kept locked now. We've never had an emergency before."

Lucy was glad that her situation warranted such a description, amazed that Health & Safety hadn't shut the place down.

She snatched the key from Melissa's hand and ran. Down dark passages, feeling her way along the closed-in walls. She found the doors, pushed the bars. The padlock and chain jammed them open at four inches.

The key, the key. Her mind screamed as she patted pockets trying to remember where she'd put it.

And then she was in the light. A high summer sun lit her path along the back alley, around the front of the building. At the corner she cast her glances furtively, like an eighties cop show. She recognised no one in the street. The grey car wasn't there. Shoulders back, skirt straightened, she sauntered across the road and into the car park.

She drove away, onto the ring road. Melissa had suggested going to Uncle Stan's. He lived on a farm, high in the hills. Lucy should go there. Melissa would try to find out what was going on and phone her later.

It was only when she got to the petrol station to fill up that Lucy remembered she'd forgotten to ask Melissa for money. She checked her wallet – a tenner and some loose change. She had a quarter of a tank. A tenner might bring her up to a half. It was hardly enough to get her to Stan's. Outside the car she leant back in, felt in all the pockets, then rifled through the glove compartment. Another two pounds. She knew her cards would be rejected.

Lucy watched the counter click up penny by penny. When she started the engine, the needle flicked momentarily to three-quarters before settling back just over the halfway mark. It would have to do.

Lucy headed to the motorway, thrusting junctions between her and Jimmy. But she had to restrain her urge to flee *too* quickly, to save petrol.

The fuel light was on as she wound through the back lanes, announcing herself to the sheep before safely rolling up outside Stan's door.

He opened his arms and ushered her in, knowing she would tell him when she was ready.

Melissa phoned two days later.

"Jimmy's been picked up."

"Is he OK? What happened?" Lucy wondered at her own concern.

"He was absent without leave. They found him sleeping on a bench in the park behind your place."

"Who? The police?"

"Sort of. Some lads were pissing about, trashing the swings, throwing stones or something. Someone called the police. Jimmy got caught up in it all. He gave his name, was flagged on the police computer and the military policemen took him away."

"Did you see him?"

"No. The police contacted me when they couldn't find you. He's left you a letter."

"Read it for me."

When Lucy put down the phone she knew it was over.

When it first ended she'd ignored his letters, let the answerphone take all his calls, and moved. He'd traced her so she moved again. And now he'd had to go AWOL because he wanted to see her, to explain how much he still loved and missed her. Her running away had shown him, finally, that she didn't feel the same way.

For some reason she couldn't fathom, Lucy felt wretched knowing Jimmy would face a court martial. But that would be easier than her telling him that she didn't love him, that she didn't care.

Later, Lucy sat in a field surrounded by contentedly grazing sheep. She plucked at the clover and wept. Stan gazed from his window, patiently waiting.

# 2005

Recycling

plus

a helmet, dancing/a disco, locked doors, and a market

# Winning Entry, 2005

Graeme Down, Aylesford, Kent

## The Jump

Fabian's gaze swept over the skips below, aligned end to end and surrounded by bored looking security. Normally filled with recyclable household waste, they stood empty and hollow, like beasts with open maws to catch the unwary. Tomorrow, one miscalculation and they might well have him for dinner.

His eyes wandered to the edge of the bluff where it dropped away into the old quarry. A young woman sat there, blonde ringlets dancing in the fitful breeze. Her legs kicked the air as she studied the scene below. As if feeling his stare, she turned and favoured him with a warm smile. He strode over.

"Good morning," he said in a soft voice that belied his blocky frame. "Not a very impressive view," he joked.

"It will be tomorrow. I'm Isabella," she introduced herself, extending one hand. Fabian took it, thought about kissing it, then decided that would be a little presumptuous.

"I work at the market, and usually bring the rubbish here at the end of the day," she explained. "So I thought I would come up today and see what's going on."

"Well, I will be here tomorrow," Fabian said, trying to impress her, whilst unsuccessfully attempting to keep the boastfulness from his voice.

"Really?" Her blue eyes widened. "Not to jump?"

"Yes." He allowed himself a self-indulgent smile.

"Will you win?" she asked excitedly.

"I might do. I have been practising for many months." He waved his hand in the direction of his sleek bike nearby. Even motionless, it radiated impressive power.

"Wow. That's fantastic. And to get a place on the film set if you win. I'd love to do that. It looks a great bike. Really... shiny."

Fabian tried not to look hurt by her superficial evaluation. He was eyeing superficial attributes himself. "And this is yours?" He indicated the battered old moped, sitting on the grass behind them.

"That's my baby. Had her four years." Her pride bemused him. It was a lopsided old wreck.

"You don't wish for a newer model?" he asked.

"Why? This one runs me around town perfectly well. Mind you, riding on yours must be an experience."

Fabian seized his opening. "I could give you a little demonstration," he offered.

Isabella's face lit up, then she hesitated. "Oh, what about my moped? Do you think it will be alright here?"

Fabian pitied the thief who would steal it, but said simply, "There is no one around."

"OK," she brightened again. "Let's go!"

For an hour they sped around the town plazas and little alleyways. As they pulled up, she shouted in his ear.

"Can I have a go?"

"I don't think it would be wise." Clearly the wrong answer. Her pout was fetching though.

He reconsidered. "Well, perhaps just a quick tour of this quiet plaza."

She wasn't bad, considering. Of course he made sure he praised her highly, telling her she was a natural, trying to improve his prospects.

As they returned to the recycling site, Fabian made his next move.

"I was wondering…"

"Yes?"

"Maybe you would like to meet up. This evening? For a drink?"

She met his gaze, and a thrill of electricity, similar to the buzz he got riding, went through him.

"I'd love to. Where?"

"How about Capelli's? The club with the large wooden doors."

"I know it. In fact it's just around the corner from my apartment. You could leave your bike there, and we could walk."

"Excellent. About 9?"

"That sounds good. See you then."


Fabian spent the rest of the day in restless anticipation. He wasn't sure this was wise given the big day tomorrow, but Isabella was a prize worth pursuing.

She was waiting outside her apartment in a shimmering dress, that, much to Fabian's approval, was fairly revealing. After dropping off his gear, and securing the bike, they strolled to the club.

The huge wooden doors were open, and the doormen ushered them inside. Down stone steps they went, the throb of music getting louder, until finally it hit them as they rounded a corner. The dance floor beyond was already packed.

"Would you care for a drink?" asked Fabian.

Isabella was really a great dancer, thought Fabian in an unfocussed way, several hours and many beers later. He swayed against the wall. A feathery touch on his arm raised him slightly from his stupor.

"Are you alright?" Isabella asked, looking concerned.

"Fine," he mumbled, tripping over an obstacle that wasn't there.

"Come on, let's go back to my place. You can crash there for the night."

Fabian had hoped to be doing more than just sleeping, but back at the apartment, Isabella rebuffed his advances.

"Oh no, no. Tonight, I don't think so," she said firmly, closing her bedroom door.

Blearily, Fabian located the couch in the lounge. His crash helmet lay on the red cushions. Collapsing onto the mattress his last coherent thought was that the jump tomorrow would surely clear any hangover.

Daylight stabbed into his skull. Groaning, Fabian extricated himself from bed and padded to the shower. Isabella was nowhere to be seen. Perhaps she had gone out to fetch breakfast, he thought hopefully.

It was only as he was dressing that he noticed something wrong. He frowned. Surely the helmet had been on the cushions last night. But why would Isabella have moved it? He hunted around the room to no effect, and then a horrifying idea struck him. He raced to the back window and peered down. His stomach churned. The bike was gone. Only an hour before the jump! How on earth was he to...? The moped!

The keys were on Isabella's dresser. Fabian vaulted the stairs two at a time.

"Come on you crate," he cursed as the moped's ignition whined lazily. On the third attempt it caught. Fabian roared away, or at least that was the plan, but he was forced to settle for a sedate meander. He chafed impotently. Too late, he thought furiously. How dare she do this to him!

Finally, he arrived at the jump site. Hundreds had gathered, and the "ooohs" and "aaahs" told him that the action had already started. He shoved his way to the front and was just about to commence an altercation with a security official when he spotted

Isabella. She was already on the ramp.

"Isabella!" he screamed.

She must have heard, for she glanced in his direction, just long enough to cause her acceleration to falter slightly. A fatal distraction. As vehicle and rider arced through the sky it was clear they weren't going to make it.

At the last possible moment, amid cries from the crowd, Isabella and motorcycle parted company. She landed heavily on the surrounding matting, whilst to Fabian's horror, the bike plummeted into the skip. The noise was cacophonous, and debris flew out. Fabian fell to hands and knees.

Isabella was up, hobbling, two marshals helping her away.

"At least she seems OK," breathed a relieved spectator next to Fabian.

"No she is not," wept Fabian brokenly. The bystander stared at him, uncomprehending.

Richard Crowhurst, Spalding, Lincolnshire


The Memory of Wood


"How did you recognise him?" Robert turned to Alan as the van drove off, carrying Gary Windsor securely back to the nick.

"I wouldn't have done, if he hadn't have taken off his helmet that precise moment."

"I wonder why he did."

Alan led his colleague to a brick-a-brac and salvage stall. The stallholder stiffened noticeably as the two policemen approached, "I've got receipts for everything you know."

"Keep you hair on Kenneth, I'm just showing PC Willard here what happened."

Kenneth didn't relax. If anything he looked even shiftier as Alan guided his colleague round the stall and past a stack of chimney pots to a pair of oak doors which had been leant up against the side of the white transit van.

Robert Willard ran his hand over the faded and flaking red paint. "Georgian aren't they?" he asked Kenneth, who shrugged a response.

"You bugger!" exclaimed Robert.

"What's up?" Alan leaned forward to inspect the hand that Robert now held upwards.

"I just got a bloody splinter of that bit of wood. There, look." Alan was laughing. "What's so bloody funny?" asked Robert, aggrieved, as he sucked the thick needle of wood from his middle finger.

"That's exactly what happened to our Mr Windsor just now. He was walking through the market with his helmet on; obviously guessed he might be recognised by someone. For some reason he was looking at these doors as I came by. He hadn't got his gloves on, and he got a splinter, just like you've just done. I guess he wasn't thinking properly. He took his helmet off to suck out the wood and I saw him. He thought about running, then I guess he realised there was nowhere to go really."

The two police officers moved through the market, stopping at the burger van.

"Two teas please love." Robert placed a few coins on the polished counter. "My shout as you're the arresting officer. I guess you need to get back to the station?"

"I will soon. I'm just going to hang around here till they find his bike."

Robert nodded then glanced at the wanted poster pasted to the green bin behind them. A poor quality photo of Gary, which had been supplied by Ann-Marie's parents, leered back at him.

"I was there the night he stabbed her, the bastard," Robert muttered.

Alan said nothing but nodded, sipping his hot tea. Robert continued, "Fortunately I didn't have to see her parents, but I was involved in the hunt for the knife. Took us three days to find it. He'd chucked it down by the riverbank. It's the only real evidence we've got: there's no witnesses.

"Mind you, you'd have thought she'd have been a bit more careful, going out with a guy like that?"

Alan glared, "What are you trying to say? That the bitch deserved it? OK, I bet she wasn't a saint, none of the slappers in Cole's at the weekend are, but to stab the poor bitch three times in the stomach? That's not on Rob, no matter how short her skirt was or who he thought she was chatting up."

Robert extended his arm to calm his friend. "I'm not saying that," he said quietly. "All I'm saying is that if you've got half a brain and you're going out with a known psycho like Gary Windsor, then you don't go putting it about on a Saturday night. Especially," he lowered his eyes, "if you're carrying his baby."

"C'mon," Alan threw his plastic cup in the bin, "I've just got a couple of questions for our friend Kenneth."

Robert retrieved the cup from the bin and put it, with his own, into the special recycling bin alongside the trailer.

"You and your bloody environmental principles," laughed Alan.

"What do you want to talk to Ken for anyway? I thought he didn't have anything to do with it. Surely your not gonna book him for selling hooky chimney pots?"

"I could do the sly old bugger. There's just something I want to check out."

Kenneth tried, unsuccessfully, to hide behind his van as the two men approached. "Can't you leave me alone? You're scaring away all my customers."

"You should attract a better class of clientele then," growled Alan.

"There's nothing wrong with my clientele. Anyway, I'd never even seen this Gary guy before today, 'cept on your posters."

"Keep you hair on," continued the policeman, "I just want to know about those doors."

"What about 'em?"

"Where'd y' get them?"

"I don't remember."

Alan raised his eyebrows and stared fixedly at Kenneth. "I thought you said you had a receipt for everything?

"Yeah, well, I do. Only, I didn't exactly buy them."

"Oh yes!"

"I didn't nick 'em or anything like that. They came out a skip. They'd have gone on the tip otherwise, and that's a nice bit of oak."

Robert snorted, "A nice bit of oak that needs some sandpaper on it."

"A skip? Where?" Alan continued, ignoring the interruption.

"I don't remember," sighed Ken. "Come off it, you think I remember every bloody skip I drive by?"

"No, just the ones you pinch stuff out of."

"They're probably the same thing," cut in Robert.

"Anyway," continued Ken as if he hadn't heard anything, "haven't you heard, recycling's all the rage these days. I'm doin' my bit for the environment."

Alan got a lift back to the station with Robert. On the way they drove past the club, now closed for refurbishment. In daylight, surrounded by scaffolding, it looked like a patient isolated in a hospital ward. Dust billowed from a blue skip as builders threw old beams down from the upper storeys.

Nobody had taken any notice at the domestic between the young girl and her boyfriend, except maybe the men who'd been eyeing up the attractive, dark-skinned young woman. Nobody saw Gary drag his girlfriend roughly down the patch of ground behind the club and throw her to the ground by the fire exit. There were no witnesses as he bent, as if to help her to her feet, and stabbed her, brutally, through the chest. Nobody saw, but the doors were there, and the wood in the doors was old. The wood remembered.

Samantha Priestley, Sheffield

## Men Come And Go, But Friends Are Forever

Caroline hadn't picked this holiday. Her friend, Stacie, the ballsy one of the two of them, had chosen it, booked it and taken over completely. The only input that seemed to be required of Caroline was to turn up at the right time, remember her passport and bikini, and make all the right noises about what a wonderful job Stacie had done organising their holiday. Of course, Caroline did all that and more. It was the way their friendship went.

Apparently the Algarve had changed quite a bit since Stacie was last here. Stacie had given Caroline the low down on this 'lovely little fishing village' they were staying in. If her memory served her well, she said, it was right up Caroline's street – unspoilt, unused, unloved by the masses and not a burger in sight. But as Caroline stood on the balcony of their apartment, hearing the endless prattle of scooters and the bars already throwing out music even though it was only 4 o'clock in the afternoon, she realised fifteen years of life rushing through these streets had taken its toll on the place.

Stacie, however, was eager to get into the mood and 'soak up the atmosphere' as she put it, and insisted the two of them head straight out to see what was on offer.

Everything, it seemed, was on offer.

They traipsed from bar to bar and eventually, to one of the many discos this 'quaint little fishing village' boasted.

Outside the nightclub girls were being sick on the

side of the road and boys, ever hopeful, were holding onto them and scraping their hair away from their faces while the girls retched into the night.

A row of motorbikes were parked, leaning like drunks, on the path outside the big wooden doors at the entrance to the club.

Caroline and Stacie queued up at the museum-like double doors and entered the disco. It was quite a sullen affair. They danced languidly while rings of men measured the potential with their eyes. Where was the beauty Caroline had been expecting? Where was the romance? It might be naïve and even a little silly, but Caroline wanted the holiday she'd read about in magazines. She wanted an experience.

Stacie got hammered. And Caroline almost had to carry her back to the apartment. Halfway there Caroline stopped by some old bins. She propped Stacie up against the recycling logo that had been freshly slapped on the side of a huge bottle bank in an attempt to boost the country's flagging quota on 'green-ness'. Caroline pushed her hands down on her knees to catch her breath and stared at the floor. Some holiday, she thought. It was always the way with her and Stacie. Caroline was always the one who had to wipe up after her friend and get her back into bed before she passed out completely. She was just realising how fed up she was of this arrangement when a motorbike pulled up in front of her. A man leaned the bike awkwardly on the curb, got off, removed his helmet and slipped it under his arm like a headless ghost.

"Are you OK?" he asked her.

Caroline glanced at Stacie dribbling beside her. What would Stacie do, she wondered, if the tables were turned? What would her faithless friend do if Caroline was out of her brains and Stacie was confronted by a drop-dead gorgeous guy on a motorbike?

She gave Stacie a gentle shove to which Stacie

answered with a set of four letter words.

The man lifted his eyebrows. "Ah," he said. "I see your friend is... she have too much to drink, eh?"

His accent alone was the most intoxicating thing Caroline had experienced so far in this place. His skin, deep caramel and faultless, ached to be touched. And his eyes... oh God his eyes!

"Yes," Caroline said shyly. "She has and I suppose I should get her back really."

The man was smiling. Men here, Caroline thought, can smell an English woman's desperation.

"You could," he said, "if you like, on the bike." He motioned to the lolling motorbike, but Caroline said that wouldn't work, where would Stacie go? The man seemed disappointed when Caroline referred to the existence of the drunk girl again.

"Yes," he said. "Problem." Then a spark seemed to go off in his head and he held up his finger in the air. "Tis OK." he said. "This your first night, yes?"

"Yes."

"Then you get your friend home now and we can meet tomorrow. I wait for you at market place. You know market?"

Caroline's insides felt like they were being liquidised as she followed his directions to the market place.

"Ten o'clock in morning," he said. "I wait for you." And he got aboard his bike again and was gone.

Caroline dragged Stacie back to the apartment where she slept. Caroline was too excited to sleep and in the morning couldn't wait to tell Stacie what had happened the night before.

"So while I was ill..." Stacie said.

"Drunk."

"...yeah whatever, you were chatting up the local talent?"

"So?"

"So, obviously you're not going to meet him."

"Why not?"

"Come on Caro, men here, in places like this, they only want one thing. Besides you don't *actually* think he'll show, do you?"

Did she? Stupid, naïve old Caroline. Had she really believed a gorgeous man like that would be interested in her, actually interested in her, and not just the sex? She made coffee for Stacie, helped her get through her hangover and let go of her silly dream. Let's face it, she thought, he was too good to be true. A guy like that would never seriously want Caroline, would he?

Ten o'clock. A man parks his motorbike and waits for the English girl to meet him. He did say ten o'clock, didn't he? By eleven he's starting to doubt himself. Maybe it was the way he spoke. Maybe she couldn't understand his hopelessly splintered English. Maybe she was drunk like her friend, but he didn't think so.

At twelve o'clock he stands by the stalls in the little market square and stares up at the beautiful sky. Why didn't she come? Why didn't they ever show up? It was always the same. They seem to like him well enough in the evening when the Mateus Rose slips through their veins, but in the bright sober morning they think better of it. They cry off. Could they sense his desperation, he wondered. Was it something in the way he stood, something in his eyes? He'd envisaged a connection being made between himself and the girl from last night. He could feel something. That something could happen. A fortnight long romance, maybe more, who knows? But she'd stood him up. Why would she do that?

He prepares to put his helmet back on and climb onto his bike. He takes one last look around the market square and then, picking up the bike, lays his foot on the pedal. He catches his reflection in his side mirror. Not too bad, he thinks. Nothing *actually* wrong with him. Still, the girl must have had a better offer.

Steve Jeanes, Brighton

## Crossing France on a Motorbike

Like many foreigners before me, I fell in love with France the moment I set foot inside its borders. Its lush countryside, its relaxed lifestyle, its gorgeous women all conspired to seduce me and fill me with a feeling of calm and well-being long missing from my life.

My friend, Max, was not so easily persuaded.

"What a dump!" he looked round the café with machine-gun eyes. Two old men in flat caps played cards at a table by the door. The barman, a filthy yellow cigarette stoppering one corner of his mouth, stared into the distance as he dried a rack of wine glasses. An ancient in greasy black suit and collar-less shirt sat in the corner squeezing dismal tunes out of an accordion, and two country girls danced slowly together to the music.

Max snorted and threw back his cognac. "It's like stepping into the nineteenth century. I'm amazed they've got electricity." He snapped his fingers imperiously at the barman. The man put down his towel and lifted the brandy bottle from its shelf.

Max is a fan of modern life. He's got no time for nostalgia or the simple things. A shame really, He has many other, more noble qualities. Max would always be my first choice of companion in a fight, for instance. He's brave and ferocious, and he'll never let you down. I just wish he'd relax more sometimes. Relax and let life just wash over him. We were in a beautiful town, with nothing more pressing to do than decide what to have for dinner, and the girl in the simple, flower-pattern dress kept sneaking glances my way, and smiling. I couldn't think of anything better. Max could though:

"Why didn't we go somewhere more exciting? Russia maybe, or Africa?" He moved our helmets off the table as the barman poured the last of the bottle's contents into our glasses. "Yeah, Africa. That would have been great." Max picked his glass up and downed the contents in one, wiping his mouth with the back of his hand.

Oh, yes, Africa. Sand and flies. Great. The bike would have loved it too, and I knew who'd be expected to keep it going. I shuddered at the thought of my baby breathing in all that grit. Max couldn't tell a carburettor from a camshaft, just sat there in the sidecar like lord of all he surveyed and left yours truly to do the grunt work. I thanked the gods of grease and piston he hadn't got his way, and instead we'd ended up in this small piece of heaven.

The trip from Calais to Normandy had been trouble-free. The weather forecast predicted a storm, but for the time being the early summer sun had beaten down from a cloudless sky that stretched from horizon to horizon. We'd arrived in Alenville early evening in time for a great supper at the more-than-comfortable hotel and our first acquaintance with the local Calvados. As night had drawn in, we'd enjoyed a glorious sunset from the balcony of our room. It silhouetted the ancient church spires and chocolate-box houses of the town, and heralded the best night's sleep in years.

The morning started wet and windy, and that, as Max said, was just the hotel room. But by the time we'd filled ourselves with croissants and litres of bittersweet coffee, it began to clear and so did our heads.

A morning ride round town confirmed my earlier impressions. As an outsider, I didn't feel completely welcome, but the place had that intangible quality I can only call 'heart'. The streets held little traffic, but bustled with the fresh faces of women and plump children making their way from charcuterie to boulangerie and on to the town square, where local farmers had set up a dozen bright-canvassed stalls to sell their produce.

I felt a deep empathy with this way of life that had continued, unchanged, for centuries, but Max found it all a big yawn.

"Hah!" he said, spitting out of the sidecar and drawing disapproving glares from an old woman cheese seller and her customers, "This is prehistoric. They're dinosaurs the lot of them. Extinction's too good!"

I bit my tongue. It doesn't pay to argue with Max when he's in this kind of mood. Anyway, something unusual had caught my attention. In one corner of the square stood a series of large wooden boxes, each with a label. My French isn't great, but I recognised at least one word – verre – glass. As I watched, a woman approached and began to take empty bottles from her bag and push them into the box. She then moved onto another and deposited several newspapers. It dawned on me that the boxes contained precious materials for re-use. Impressive, and my respect for the town grew. I couldn't help thinking it wouldn't hurt some of my own countrymen to be so conscientious in these difficult times.

"Look, Max. That's hardly the act of a dinosaur. These people are thinking of the future."

He looked and snorted. "Pathetic. They'll be saving their own shit for the vegetables next."

Not such a bad idea, and one that had proved successful in the past, but I didn't fancy the argument. Meanwhile, he'd taken to licking his lips.

"Look, there's a bar. Time, I think, to wet the old whistle again, eh?"

So we'd settled in for what looked like being a long session.

Max signalled for more brandy, and nodded at the wall calendar.

"June 5th. Big day tomorrow. We should celebrate."

The barman brought the empty bottle.

"I will have to go to the cellar to get another, monsieur."

Max slapped him on the shoulder, rather too hard.

"Go, patron, go!"

With the tiniest hesitation, the man headed for the padlocked double doors at the end of the bar. As he did, the girl in the flower dress winked openly at me. I nudged Max. The girls giggled as we gave them the once over.

I think the nervous flick of her eyes warned me. Something was wrong. I turned in time to see the landlord unhitch the padlock and duck behind a table. The doors burst open and a storm of bullets blasted from dark figures lurking inside. Old instincts don't fail you. I dived sideways for cover, but too late. I hit the wall with blood pumping from my neck, knowing it was all over for me.

Max needed more convincing. I saw at least a dozen impacts stiffen his body as he scrabbled for his weapon and screamed at the top of his voice until the gush of blood from his mouth silenced him. As he spun backwards to crash over a waiting table, the Luger clattered to the ground from lifeless fingers, his final scream, "The Fuhrer will avenge me," left hanging in the air like a ghost.

There are worse places to die. But I'd have loved the chance to celebrate my 18th birthday tomorrow in the peace of this Normandy countryside, so far from the war.

Shelley Ellerbeck, London

Retiring?

As she walked up to the ornate timber doors, she could feel her heart beating. God, how she hated these occasions, especially when she had to come on her own. 'Speed Dating,' they called it. Five minutes to introduce yourself to someone, say something interesting, which would make them want to spend eternity with you, then move on. And again. Ad infinitum. A little like life, she thought, as the door swung open and a gloved hand appeared, proffering a tray of champagne. The venue looked a bit posh, shame Linda hadn't been able to come. She would be able to tell her all about it next week. Make her jealous. That would serve her right for letting her down at the last minute... Who was this disabled aunt she had to visit anyway? Sounded like a poor excuse to Claire. She stepped in.

"Would madam like to go through?" The waiter's voice was polished, smooth. Years of talking to people he didn't give a monkey's about, thought Claire, smiling politely.

*Madam would prefer to be boiled in oil, whilst listening to Barry Manilow,* she thought. But all she said was:

"Thank you."

As soon as she entered, she knew something was amiss. Heavy chandeliers cast bejewelled shadows across embroidered drapes. Sedate groups of people sipped drinks and made polite conversation. Claire glanced at the antique mirror over the marble fireplace. Great: she looked like Lily Savage with sunburn. Where were all the desperate-looking women dancing round their handbags? The men nursing bottles of beer? Why did everyone look as though they had just jetted back from the Bahamas? And where was the disco? This was one hell of an upmarket speed dating evening. She gulped down her glass of champagne in one, then grabbed a second from a passing tray. Desperately trying not to sneeze with the intake of bubbles through her nose, Claire put her tongue up to the roof of her mouth. Linda's failsafe remedy to avoid sneezing in an inappropriate place. A bluff voice interrupted her manoeuvres:

"Exquisite detail on the ceiling, isn't it. I love to gaze up at it myself. Lifts the spirits, I'd say. Somewhat reminiscent of a Renaissance church, don't you think?"

"Er, yes, it is." Claire was a little lost for words as she looked up. The voice she was listening to possessed vowel sounds she had only ever heard in the Queen's speech. "It's beautiful." She sneezed.

"Quite." A large, freckled hand shot out to shake hers. She found herself looking into an earnest pair of blue eyes. Not another insurance salesman... "And what do you do? I don't think I've seen you before."

"I'm in recycling," Claire said brightly, sniffing. How could she tell someone who sounded like royalty that she was one of the few female 'dustmen' in London? He would probably faint. Linda would have told him outright, exaggerating her Cockney twang for the occasion, but Claire didn't quite have her confidence.

"Recycling?" His brow furrowed: "I didn't know we did recycling. Fascinating. How long have you known Henry, then?"

"Henry?"

"Yes, Henry." He licked his lips. "Nothing like a glass of Bolly to muddle a girl's spirits, what? Henry. The chap who's retiring. You know, thirty years in the marketplace and all that?"

Claire recovered her wits: "Oh, Henry! *That* Henry, of course!" These people knew each other! Were they all speed dating from the same company? She would kill Linda. Ah well, she would bluff it out for a while. There would be plenty to talk about on Monday. That was for sure.

"The name's Giles, by the way. And you are...?"

"Claire."

"Claire, from Recycling. Super."

Claire tried desperately to think of something interesting to say: "So Henry's been in the marketplace for thirty years, has he? Amazing. Such a long time to have a stall. He must have seen some changes."

"Oh yes." Giles' face showed puzzlement, albeit briefly. "Best trader we've seen for a long time. He even came through Black Wednesday relatively unscathed. Did that affect you bods in Recycling?"

Claire racked her brains. "Black Wednesday? Not really." What on earth was the man talking about? They collected black bags on a Wednesday, after green boxes on a Monday and brown bins on a Tuesday, but how could he know that? She decided to change the subject. "So which market do you work on, Giles?"

"I deal with the Far East and Asia. Thrilling work, as you can imagine. Especially in the present climate."

Claire nodded in what she hoped was a wise way. Chinese bags and Asian jewellery were in at the moment, so he must be making a packet. How he managed to attract any trade with that accent was hard to imagine though. Maybe he changed it for work? Their conversation was interrupted by the sound of tapping. Was that the sign to move on to the next partner and start again? No one seemed to be moving, so she stayed where she was.

There were cries of "Speech!" and a grey-haired man

came up to the front of the room. This was unusual. Maybe he would explain about moving on.

He cleared his throat: "First of all, I would like to thank you all for coming to my retirement bash. Here at Goodman Sox, we pride ourselves on..."

Shit, she was in the wrong place, big time. Goodman Socks? Wasn't that the new retail outlet near Bermondsey? A retirement do? She would kill Linda on Monday, she would. Claire decided now was the time to leave quietly. She would head for the back of the room while everyone was listening to the speech, then escape through any door she could find.

As she started to wend her way towards the exit, she was vaguely aware of a commotion at the front of the room. Laughter, followed by a collective gasp. She stopped and turned round. After all, whatever was happening, it would be something else to tell Linda.

The sight that greeted her eyes was bizarre, to say the least. Someone in a black helmet and motorbike leathers had appeared next to the man making the speech. Some kind of courier, it looked like, unzipping his jacket. Well, it was hot. Another intake of breath. Under the jacket she could see a tasselled bra and a flat, pierced stomach. The rest of the leathers came off and the body began to gyrate around the poor man, who by this time had turned puce. Great! Someone had decided to get him a strippergram! After thirty years selling socks, he deserved that. Claire decided to stay and watch the fun, already planning how she would tell the story next week.

As she moved forward for a better view, she found herself feeling a little sad that Linda couldn't be there to watch. She would have loved all this. The bra came off. French manicured hands reached up to take off the helmet.

As the woman looked up at the crowd, smiling, her eyes caught Claire's. A vague feeling of recognition pierced the champagne-induced haze. *Bloody hell! Linda!* That was when Claire hit the floor.

Sarah Thompson, Moss Vale, Australia

Just Desserts

John was in the middle of reaching his greatest achievement in his long history of picking up chicks at a bar when his phone rang. He looked down at the caller ID and saw that it was Eric.

"Yeah, John here."

"Oh thank God you answered. We need to meet."

"Eric, this is not a good time! I was just about to go home for coffee with two *beautiful* young ladies."

John looked at the two girls in front of him as they gave him an approving smile.

"Come on John, this is urgent."

"All right, all right, keep your wig on. When and where?"

"Now. I'm at the recycling plant, and I've got an urgent job."

John looked at his watch, 12.15am.

"Alright, I'll be there in ten."

He looked at the two girls and shrugged his shoulders, then headed towards the front door, collecting his helmet from the front desk on the way out. John jumped on his motorbike and sped dangerously through the deserted city streets. It took only five minutes for him to reach the recycling plant, where Eric was already waiting.

"Took your time didn't you?"

"Huh! Come on then, let's have it."

"Right then, here's the file." Eric passed John a green manila folder. John took the folder and began to look over its contents.

"It's a business competitor my client doesn't want around anymore," began Eric. "It's a simple job, shouldn't take you more than half an hour if all goes to plan. He'll be at the open air markets on Norton Street tomorrow, he goes there every Saturday at the same time to buy fresh ingredients – he's a keen chef you know? Anyway, my client needs it done this weekend and no later. Can you do it?"

John looked over the picture and read the name out loud. "George Percy?"

"Yeah, so what of it."

"Oh nothin. It's just... well. Oh nothin, I think I'm gettin him confused with someone else. All right, it looks easy enough, I'm in."

"OK, well I gotta go, got another job to set up for next week in Madrid. You know how it is, there's always someone who wants someone dead."

John laughed as he turned to get back on his bike. He put on his helmet and sat down, then turned to Eric and said, "you know, I feel like there's somethin I should remember about this bloke."

"Don't worry about it John, this time tomorrow it won't matter anyway will it? I mean, he won't be around to remind you will he? Go back to your girls."

John gave Eric a wave as he sped away and headed up the dark alleyway and into the night.

The next morning John slowly slid himself out of bed, and looked for his watch among the clothes which were scattered across a sea of marine blue carpet. 10.20am.

"Better hurry or I'll miss this George bloke."

John rushed his clothes on and was just opening the door when he heard a voice from behind.

"I'll ah, I'll call you", stammered John as he ran down the stairs and into the street.

When John arrived at the designated place shortly after, everything was all as he was told. George Percy

194

came trundling along, oblivious to what was about to happen. John pulled the telescope to his eye, and aimed the rifle at his target by a produce stall in the market below.

"Bloody people, get out of the road. Nothin I can't stand worse than a bunch of people gettin in my road when I'm trying to make a hit. Ah, here we go."

Cool as ice, John pulled the trigger and watched his man go down. Without a second glance he packed the rifle back into his briefcase and calmly walked away, job done and ready to head home for a nice cup of tea.

Within ten minutes of leaving the market, John pulled up in front of his studio apartment.

"What the bloody hell is this then?" screeched John as he discovered a thick chain and padlock barring his entry. "Who in God's name...?"

John grabbed a hand-written notice from the wall beside the door.

"Due to lack of rental payments made, you have been evicted. Any attempts to enter these premises will result in a visit from the police, and an uncomfortable night in the nick. Have a nice life.

Signed Harry Thompson.

(Landlord)"

"Great, just great. Where the hell am I meant to go now? Back to the girls' flat? No bad idea. Ahh, I know who'll take me in."

Without a second thought John rode the five blocks to his ex-girlfriend Kerry's house. When he arrived, he saw Kerry standing outside her door fishing for her keys.

"Kerry... baby."

"Oh what the hell are you doing here?"

"Come on baby, don't be like that."

"I'll be any bloody way I feel. Now what are you doing here?"

"I need somewhere to stay the night."

"No! No way."

"Come on Kerry, it's just one night. I got evicted today."

"Again?"

"I promise it's just for tonight, you see I'm a bit strapped for cash at the moment, but I'm gettin a big pay tomorrow, and don't worry I'll fix you up for lettin me stay. What do you say?"

Kerry rolled her eyes and gave him a wave to come in. "Come on then. And don't be messing the place up or you'll be out on your arse."

"No, of course not. But do you reckon I could grab a shower, I'm a bit grubby."

"Yeah, you know where the bathroom is."

"Oh, and a cup of tea would be great too, thanks. I'll have it when I'm finished up in here."

Kerry flipped her middle finger up at John as he shut the bathroom door behind him. As soon as she heard the shower start she lunged forward to where the briefcase was and began to pry it open. Within a minute she was inside and discovered the rifle. That didn't surprise her, because she knew what John did, but when she got to the file and saw the photo her mouth dropped. Just then, she was distracted by a news flash coming from the TV.

Twenty minutes later John turned off the hot water and dried himself off. He wrapped the towel around his waist and smiled when he put the radio on. "And today's breaking news... prominent businessman George Percy was gunned down in Norton Street markets at 10.45 this morning—"

"You made that tea yet...?" he called out as he opened the bathroom door.

He looked up just in time to see a copper hurling his large body towards him. With a huge thud, both he and the policeman landed on the polished wooden floorboards, and his hands were cuffed from behind. John looked up at Kerry, who was standing above him with an angry expression on her face.

"Why, Kerry? Why?"

"Do you remember a few months ago when you asked me if I was dating anyone?"

"Oh bullocks, I knew there was something about that bloke I needed to remember."

# 2004

Global Warming

plus

a hostage, a tarantula, a rocket, and a swimming pool

# Winning Entry, 2004

Steve Jeanes, Brighton

## Getting It

"Global warming!"

"What?"

"Global warming! It says in the paper global warming's responsible for all the freak weather we've been having."

*Cobblers*, thought Eddie, *no such thing*. He stood back to admire his work. The huge 4x4 glowed malevolently in its garage. Eddie reached forward and rubbed one final speck of polish from its gleaming shell. His reflection smiled back at him, satisfied. He was tempted to kiss it.

"You little beauty. You ain't never going near no mud, I promise." He dropped the rag on a bench, and, with one final backward glance headed off for brunch.

"They'll be telling us the country's gonna be full of poisonous spiders next!" He yelled in the general direction of the patio, where Una, be-curlered and still in her dressing-gown sat sipping champagne and chomping burgers as she leafed through the Sundays.

"Well, it does say there's some kind of killer virus getting into swimming pools. Have we had the pool cleaned recently?" Her screech battered Eddie's ears as he flip-flopped his way to the white cast-iron table. "Oh, you're here."

"Yes, I'm here. Gimme one of them burgers, babe." He snatched one from the stack and lashed it with ketchup and mayonnaise before sitting and grabbing a tabloid.

"Well have we?"

"What?"

"Had the pool cleaned?"

"Yeah, yeah."

"When?"

Eddie tried to chew and swallow simultaneously.

"Look, you don't wanna believe any of that old bollocks. They makes it all up, don't they? There's always one thing or another."

Una sniffed and picked a thin sliver of dill pickle from under one carmine nail.

"We-ell."

"Stands to reason, don't it? They got to make up stuff to sell the papers. I mean, look at this one here," Eddie prodded the page with the remains of his burger, smearing it with gore. "Rocket launch goes wrong. This thing's not got into orbit proper and they reckon there's bits going to come crashing down all over the place. I ask you, what a load of old—"

"Yeah, but some of it's got to be true, hasn't it?"

"Hah. Even the weather's only right half the time – and they're *trying* to tell the truth then." Eddie filled his plate again, and belched contentedly.

"Manners!"

"Yeah, yeah. Ha! Look! Another one!" he waved the paper in front of her, making her flinch back from the image of the bound and gagged man. "Now they're saying there's this gang of terrorists going round picking on random targets. Just trying to put the fear up us, that's all, innit? I mean, why would a bunch of towel-heads want to pick on ordinary God-fearing people like us, eh?"

Una batted the paper away.

"Well I don't know, maybe they just don't like us."

"Oh, you daft cow," Eddie slapped the paper down

and picked up his beer. "You was always two bricks short of a bungalow. What's not to like?" He looked around, admiring his domain. The six bedroom mock-Tudor residence with its drive and electric wrought-iron gates, the three-car garage, the Olympic-sized pool, the mighty gas-powered barbecue, the huge lawn with its built-in putting green where his two pedigree Dobermans were fighting over the remains of a rabbit, Una herself with all her expensive additions and improvements. He'd done good. The second-hand car business had seen him all right, with the help of a few little deals on the side. He'd had to work hard, and a few awkward bastards had tried to queer the pitch, but he'd seen them all off, one way or another. He was a self-made man who'd got where he was from the sweat of his own labours. What was there not to like? He let out another contented belch.

"Scuse *I*."

Una screwed up her £2000 nose.

"I hope you're not going to keep doing that when the Reynolds come round this afternoon."

"Aaaah, shit!" He'd forgotten all about the neighbours coming. He picked up his beer and chugged it back, trying to wash the sour taste from his mouth. "Waddya have to go and invite them round again for?"

"Well, it's only polite. They had us round for Corinne's birthday, and we couldn't really ignore them any longer, hun." Una gave him that sad puppy look, but he wasn't having any.

"I don't mind *her*. She's a good laugh, and that's a cracking rack on her, but him! Him and his bloody solar panels and compost heap, he needs a good kick up the arse." Eddie went to swig the bottle, found it empty and chucked it in the hydrangea. There was a chink as it found the pile. "Get us another one, doll." She scowled and flounced off through the French windows. "And if he mentions re-bloody-cycling once," he yelled after her receding back, "I promise, this time I'll chuck him in the bloody pool, killer bug or not!"

Una re-appeared with the bottle, levering the top off as she walked.

"He's all right. You just wind him up, that's all. Just because he doesn't know anything about football or cars or gambling. I like him."

Eddie grabbed the bottled and chucked it back in one.

"He's a tosser. A grade one bloody middle-class woolly-brained tosser. If he wasn't a neighbour..." Eddie left the thought hanging as he stood up and stripped off his top. "Just make sure you get rid of them before final score, right?"

Una stuck her tongue out and gave Eddie the finger as he stepped out of his flip-flops and waddled towards the pool.

The coroner had never seen a crowd like it. Flashguns popped in all directions as he tried to make his announcement.

"Was it the spider?"

"Was it the debris?"

"Please, please, be patient. I know this incident has caused an unusual amount of interest—"

"Too right mate. Billion to one chance, at least. So which one killed him? My money's on the terrorist sniper."

"No! It was the freak bolt of lightning!"

"Please gentlemen! And ladies of course. I'm getting to it."

"Was it the virus in the pool?"

"People! People! Please! He was dead before he hit the virus-riddled water. That he was bitten by a poisonous spider, hit by a sniper's bullet, a freak bolt of lightning and a piece of space debris simultaneously, is irrelevant. None of these things killed Eddie Pascoe.

The crowd muttered amongst itself unhappily, deprived of the headline they were looking for, or had already prepared.

"What did he die of then?"

"His heart just stopped moments before. Just as he was diving."

"His heart stopped? Why?"

"Uh, yes, that's where it gets difficult really. This isn't an exact science. There've been a lot of theories bandied about both in the press and at my office, but nothing concrete."

"What do you think it was then?"

"What do I think? I think my assistant, Lizzie's theory is as good as any."

"Yeah? And what does this Lizzie have to say then?"

The mob of reporters pressed forward as one. The corner of the coroner's mouth twitched momentarily.

"Lizzie? Hrrmph, well, Lizzie says he was asking for it."

Laura Dawn, Billericay

## Whitewash

The engines of the plane groaned in a tangible, though nearly inaudible rumbling. The noise wormed its way to dwell in the man's innermost ear and brain, making them simmer and pop. Occasional gusts of strong wind rattled the metal fuselage like a demand for freedom from within a jailor's cage. It was bright, horribly, artificially bright inside. No window could let in air – or even the plastic pretence of daylight caught at that strange angle peculiar to aeroplanes. Just huge expanses of white; padded walls and a hard grey floor made up the entire interior. The cleanliness, the motion and the air were all oppressive, depressive, nauseating.

Guy was not directly bothered by any of these circumstances. His concentration was within. It must be so, if a political prisoner is not to run mad. With the utmost exertion of willpower, he tried to ignore the sickening wedge in his mouth. The astringent taste and ceaseless pressure reminded him of a dentist mercilessly taking impressions of his teeth for a brace as a boy. Condemned to a dentist's chair for the ten, or ten million, hours it felt he was doomed to spend in this plane. Those captors really knew what they were doing.

No less torturous were the cord bindings around his wrists. Guy could feel them cutting ruts into his tender skin. He could not move his hands for fear of embedding the ties deeper, and a strange and painful numbness had taken over his two arms.

Singularly, Guy could possibly endure either of his trials, but for a recent addition to his luxury cabin. Admittedly it was a novelty, but it was not one which stood in danger of amusing him for long. Pleasure in gaining something to look at rapidly ebbed away as it scuttled closer and closer. A whopping great spider. How could those things be so ugly?! All made of black sinewy gunge. Guy's hunger flew out, as if with the wind sailing past the plane, to see eight hideous arched legs moving in a frenzied, clicking little dance across the floor.

This companion was not assigned to him by his friendly neighbourhood captors. It was not launched upon him from a trapdoor, but oozed itself out of a minuscule crack between him and the cargo. A stowaway. See, this is what these guys should be worrying about, thought Guy. Look at that thing! It had green hair, like mould had set in upon its repulsive back; probably had fangs too, and would reproduce like a rabbit on speed. How many crops could that thing infect, devastate with the hard-to-pronounce foreign disease it was sure to smuggle in? That bugger would kill. Instead they were bearing down upon *him*: a harmless, though intelligent guy, not strong, or rich, or with anything to his name but a Maths and Astrophysics degree. It made him sick. As sick as the increasingly erratic bumping of the plane, and gag in his mouth taking away his freedom of speech.

But the gag was the least of his worries now. Guy's skin itched with the proximity of the spider as it edged its way closer like an alien craft approaching his leg. There *were* fangs. Guy saw them glint in the light. A sudden buffet of wind bounced it within a centimetre of him. A shudder of horror rippled all through Guy. Unable to move at all, he closed his eyes tight and braced himself.

But the bite never came. Something had happened to

the aircraft, for the next thing Guy felt was the impact of his head against one of the walls. A bang of sound burst in his eardrum with such painful ferocity that the whole of his head was set ringing. A sting of cool, sharp air pushed against his face. Bright, blinding light exploded before his eyes, and then he saw no more.

When Guy awoke, the only sensation he could feel was cold. One entire half of his face was numbed solid. It was pressed against something very wet with pointed, icicle fingers. An arctic breeze was ravishing his back, as well as his hands tied there.

But the gag was gone. He could taste a crystal liquid, and feel something wet trickling out of the corner of his mouth. Slowly he raised his pounding head.

White. Another expanse of white, this time on a grander scale, ranging further than the eye could see, pure, virginal, natural white. None of your false neon lights here. This was the grandeur of nature; cobalt blue water, rolls upon rolls of a winter wonderland, magnificent mountains of an odd gnarled shape. And it was bloody cold.

Though he could not think through the fog in his head, he obeyed the single instinct which took possession of him: run. Stumbling to his knees, then with difficulty to his feet, he ran. He ached with cold. Every joint had stiffened, and protested against movement. His legs dragged along, crunching and squelching in the snow. Had he possessed all his usual strength, he would not get along much faster. Each step plunged deep in snow, or slid in ice beneath him. He was hurdling, not walking. And all the while he could hear the grunting, mournful squeal of aircraft wheeling round in the white spotted air.

Where to hide on a stretch of cotton landscape, where he was a dot of ink on a white shirt? He, Guy, an innocent man, a man of genius! He did not deserve such an end. What kind of uncultured, savage people would deprive the world of a brain like his?

His barbaric jailers were upon him once more. A smudging shadow trickled towards him over the ice. Guy, half falling, half sinking, struggled onwards. The hum of the planes grew louder and louder until it suddenly burst forth in a whine and a thud. Close by him a shower of snow splintered upwards in the air. Another to his left. Another far in front. Bullets.

The last shot was aimed ridiculously wide of him. Guy almost laughed at the aim until a jolt beneath his feet made him stop dead and raise his eyes. The ridge before him was trembling, disintegrating in a sharp quiver under his nose. An avalanche. He stood, awe-struck to see what one bullet could do to this strong, compact snow. Bloody Global Warming.

Quick as a deer Guy turned and darted in a desperate bid to escape the powder descending upon him. It did not matter if he died. He had what they wanted, not just caught in the intricate maze of his mind, but on paper. They did not know he had the papers that someone, someday, could still find.

Falling off his feet, Guy reached the edge of his slab of ice. An immense cliff, sparkling and brilliant, reached down into dazzlingly blue water. It was like a huge magical swimming pool, winking to him from far below. Guy paused for a moment, and jumped.

He fell in a great splash into the freezing water just as half of the iceberg collapsed. Mini-earthquakes cracked along it, and the heap of sliding snow came crashing down in a crescendo. He did not emerge from the wreckage.

Yet later, out in the ocean, a sealed package of paper bobbed its way to the surface: his precious plans. His plans for an atomic rocket which could cause similar devastation not just to this planet, but to the Universe.

Anuradha Choudry, Pondicherry, India

Imprisoned – For Life

It had started flashing across the television screen a week back – "Global Warming Reaches Alarming Rates!" Even reports of the devastation caused by the Tsunami had been taken over by the soaring temperatures and forest fires.

Dr. Harrison Freeman watched the news with concern. He had all the riches and success that he had dreamt of achieving as a passionate young man. Many of his colleagues envied the heights he had reached in his profession, and yet here he was... powerless to change a thing!

Every front page and every news channel had its own explanation for what could have contributed to the prairie fires. Dr Freeman was convinced it was global warming. Some serious action had to be taken immediately to combat the looming threat. If only his colleagues would listen to him! For the past week he'd had the same heated discussions with them as he heard on the TV debates.

"We have to take URGENT steps to reverse climate change – starting with drastic cutbacks on heavy industrialisation!"

"You want to take us back to the dark ages! Who's going to put up with that?!"

"No," he retorted. "We need to use more technology, not less! Environmentally friendly technology to *reduce* CFCs and other greenhouse gases—"

"Yeah, you talk big, like all the environmentalists, but in the end it's simple: there's a price to pay for progress."

"Price?! If we fail to respect the balance of nature soon, we'll sure pay the price! – our human existence on this earth!"

The environmentalists had long back figured it out. Indiscriminate deforestation throughout the globe was a prime cause of global warming. Had they not emphasised often enough the importance of conserving rainforests?

"Yeah, we all respect the balance of nature! My wife put some new plant pots out in our yard: that'll do our bit for global warming this year!"

Even though being 'environmentally-friendly' was the trend of the day, how many people were truly concerned about conservation in their daily life, asked Ms. Alyna Green, the reputed environmental activist, on TV. She had given a cynical smile on Larry King Live and said, "It's too late now!"

Dr Freeman had recently become convinced of the urgent need to investigate the impact of atmospheric temperatures on sea levels – what would happen if the ice-caps started melting with a momentum that couldn't be reversed? Now that the facilities at Cape Canaveral had been flattened by the Florida Tsunami, the launch of the new international mission had been transferred to Alaska: what impact would that have on the ice-caps – would it be enough to imbalance the Arctic temperatures? The repercussions could be disastrous.

"We need to postpone the launch!" he had told his deputy.

Not everyone has direct access to the President, but the Director of the NASA Space Programme can get through immediately when he insists that it is a matter of national security.

"I know this launch is as important to you as it is to

me, Mr President, but this time we have to postpone it until we can carry out further investigations."

But not everyone can persuade the President of their concerns in five turbulent minutes.

"Now that's final, Harrison! This is a unique mission for peace, and it has taken years of work to get the Iraqi astronaut ready! I've told you before, this launch is crucial for my image ahead of the Middle East talks next month. And I don't need my Space Director of all people joining the 'Green Gold' movement."

Dr Freeman had been forced to hang up, cursing the risk the world was taking for the benefit of one man's megalomania.

Now he looked at the television again, and noticed that the 'Global Warming' logo of the earth on fire seemed to have been assigned a permanent corner on the screen. He was worried.

Yesterday's news was still weighing on his mind. And his only companion, a tarantula in its transparent aquarium tank, was not in the least concerned, just like his colleagues – only adding to his frustration.

He was not against the launch itself – the project was his brainchild after all. That was why he had sent several proposals to the Pentagon and other Government departments suggesting they merely postpone the scheduled launch.

No one was interested!

A week ago he had confided in a friend that he was thinking of issuing a press statement in a last bid to win public support for further investigations into atmospheric temperatures. But he had not been able to go through with it in the end.

His utter powerlessness was killing him. He was trying to stay awake in his chair by keeping his eyes glued to the television: he was afraid of sleeping. Yes, afraid of the nightmare that had come back, not once, not twice, but every night for the past week – he had dreamt of that monster-wave mercilessly smashing everything in its way.

He had been there in Florida at the time, and the Tsunami was coming back to haunt him.

But there was a sinister difference with this wave, which made his limbs cold and lifeless. And unlike the Tsunami, when the sea had done her destruction and left her ruins, this wave came to stay. He frantically searched for survivors but they had all been swallowed up by the flooding sea level, leaving only a deathless silence to accompany the unbearable heat of the sun.

Although he was trying not to sleep, he must have dozed off for a few seconds when the loud shrieks of children playing outside had startled him to wakefulness. He knew there was a pool in the garden because, from his chair, he had seen its reflection on the mirror that hung on the angled eaves above the attic window. As he woke he caught a glimpse of himself in the other mirror, a full-length Victorian piece covered in a layer of dust where local spiders had excelled in their craftsmanship of web designing. A helpless Dr Freeman stared back at him.

Then the tarantula caught his eye: it had become abnormally restless and was scrabbling against the walls of its prison. Maybe he's finally protesting at the launch, he thought ironically, as the rolling news channel started showing more replays of yesterday's event.

It must have been only a minute before he heard the familiar roaring again. He tried hard to push the sound out of his head but it only got overwhelmingly louder. He opened his eyes and looked at the mirror for reassurance when something slammed hard on the building. The mirror on the wall fell, and the sound of its shattering was lost in the deafening roar.

Was he dreaming again? Or...?

He closed his eyes and did what was left for him to do. He prayed.

When he opened his eyes the TV had blanked out. The familiar deathless silence greeted him. He looked at himself in the cracked Victorian mirror. And smiled. Yes, in spite of the gag, he smiled. He imagined the devastation at his sea-view apartment, and could picture the articles in the next day's papers – 'Dr. Harrison Freeman and a Tarantula – Bound to Live!' and 'Imprisoned – For Life!'

# A 15-photo story

Dan Lamb, London

## A Passing Pit Stop in the Night

The sudden approach of an engine gave only a moment's warning before a motorbiker burst through the firmly shut side doors of the quiet pub. As he skidded to a halt amongst the debris of bar stools, he hurled his helmet down onto the bar: it bounced off the surface and rolled into a pile of dirty glasses, sending them splintering onto the ground and drawing a squeal from the teenage barmaid.

Life simply wasn't as good in England as she had dreamed of when she had come over from Bulgaria.

"Where's the landlord?" the intruder demanded. "I'll tie him up if he doesn't pay back what he owes me!"

So much for all her dreams, as a summer nanny for the children of rich British families: while they had played in the swimming pools of their rented holiday villas she was continually practising her English with high hopes of eventually 'making it' with a good job.

She wished the biker *would* tie the landlord up; she felt like a hostage herself, stuck in this pub all hours with no money and only a dirty lodging upstairs. And her wages were kept at least a month in arrears to make sure she didn't go doing a runner.

"I'm sorry sir," she replied timidly. "He's not here at the moment."

"What do YOU want!" the biker growled at the one nervous customer who had chivalrously got up from his table in the corner to help the barmaid out. "You think I'm gonna be scared of you! And you, bitch!" – he turned back to the bar, where he had thrown his helmet. "Tell him I'll be back for that and I want it full to the brim of used twenties. And don't even think of calling the cops because I'll tell you now, you won't be doing your boss any favours."

The man dressed in tattoo sleeves pays for his petrol through the night kiosk with a scowl and the attendant is left behind his counter alone to pass the time. It's a long shift ahead, with plenty of verbal abuse to look forward to later when all the drunks come past for cigarettes on their winding way home.

The time passes slowly when there are so few customers. But at least he'll have the chance to look at his revision notes for the exam next week. He steps out for a breath of fresh air while there are no cars on the forecourt and spots a shooting star, which he convinces himself is the latest rocket sent into orbit to bring much-needed supplies to the international space station: as seen on TV earlier.

Gazing longingly up into the sky he trips over the long ladder that has been left out the back: he's just about to put it away when he hears his mobile ringing inside. He's not supposed to leave his phone on – there are signs everywhere for customers saying they are a danger – but he hasn't blown the petrol pumps up yet, so he's not planning to turn it off until his supervisor is due in the morning.

Missed call...! One of his university friends' numbers – it's not likely to be important and anyway he doesn't want to waste his credit ringing back. The beep of a text message comes through. *When ru gona quit that job in the global warming biz n join us 4 sum fun on a sat nite?* His eyes linger on the attached picture of two girls dancing in a club: they zoom up nicely until he is distracted by a biker revving up to one of the pumps.

"What's happened to those doors?" rages the landlord. "Are we supposed to use that as an emergency exit now or what?!" His forearms are

216

shaking so much with anger that the tattoos engraved there appear to have become dancing girls.

His tearful barmaid tries to explain the traumatic event to him. "Shall I call the police?" she asks.

"No chance!" he menaced with finality. "We don't want them poking their noses into anything!" He looked around at the completely empty bar, aware that business would be even slower when word of this got about. "When's he coming back?" he growled.

"He didn't say when... but I assume he's coming tonight."

"OK, I'm going upstairs to call the big boys. I'll put the readies in his helmet and leave it behind the bar with you... just hand it over when he gets here."

England was supposed to be such a civilised country, full of strawberries and cream. She thought she'd have left all the mafia and underworld behind when she came here to seek her fortune.

There were no customers. A Saturday night had never been so quiet before. At least the glasses were all spotless by the time the motorbiker returned.

"You pass on my message?" he growled at her.

She nodded, and bent down behind the bar to pick up his package. The biker stood on guard, ready for a trap, but she re-appeared with his helmet stuffed full.

"The whole amount?" he demanded, not taking his level gaze away from the scared bright blue mirrors which were anything but a reflection of his own soulless eyes. "I know where to find you if it isn't," he threatened, turning so suddenly that one of the twenty pound notes fluttered off the top of the pile and floated out of his reach behind the bar. "One for yourself, luv," he said nonchalantly, in too much of a hurry to stop.

As soon as he was out of the front door, she picked up her coat and rucksack that she'd hidden in the large swing bin, and tiptoed towards the new emergency exit. And when she heard the commotion she was expecting out the front, she ran. Out of the motorbike-shaped hole in the side doors, across the car park, and anywhere the road would take her.

The commotion had grown louder, and it sounded like a fairer fight than she had anticipated, with several on each side. She just needed to get to the petrol station up ahead.

Breathless, she ran straight to the kiosk and pounded on the glass. The attendant immediately picked up a key and gestured at her with it to come around to the back. He had the door open, slammed and locked before he'd said a word.

"Is someone chasing you?"

She nodded, throwing down her bag and unbuttoning her coat as she slumped on the floor.

"Who is it? Let me call the police."

"No—" she yelped. "Promise me you won't call them – not until the morning!"

"The morning?" he wondered, considering the possibilities of what she had in mind. "You can't stay here! – unless you let me call the police. I can't afford to get in any trouble."

As her breathing settled into a calmer rhythm, she stood up. "Then there must be somewhere I can hide!" she appealed with all the brightness of her pretty face.

He considered silently for a moment, and thought of the ladder.

"What about the roof?" she said slowly, her eyes clearly capable of searching out his deepest thoughts.

He looked at her clothes – their quality as cheap as the tops at the market that even the poorest of his student friends turned their noses up at.

"Let me make you a cup of tea first, while we check the coast is clear," he offered. "And then I'll lend you my coat."

*

"My supervisor will be on her way soon; you definitely can't stay any longer."

Once they had started chatting, there just hadn't been a convenient point to stop, all the way through to the morning. In the middle of the night she had offered to climb onto the roof but got the message when he laughed about the nest of tarantulas that he said he'd found up there when he'd once had to go up to retrieve a kid's frisbee.

"See that bench over there by the traffic lights, on the other side of the road? Take my coat, and wait for me there until my boss arrives, I won't be long. I can make sure you do better than this dump of a town, I promise..."

He made the call from his mobile. "Yes, you heard me right. A taxi to London, please." Then he replied to his friend: *think i hav dun beta here than u in the club, or hav i just been dreaming?* He would send them a picture message from Big Ben to prove it.

It was when she had showed him the stash of money she had taken from her landlord's till and from the bottom of the biker's helmet that he realised he had fallen for her. Recycling empty crisp packets, she'd called it. And it was when the hay-laden farm truck pulled away from the traffic lights to reveal the empty bench that he realised he would never see her again. But he would always remember her name.

Also published by Fygleaves: New authors revealing
their leaves to the world

THE MYTHS OF TURRET ROCK

BY DAN LAMB

The author of our 15-photostory, A Passing Pit Stop in the Night, is
a self-confessed writing addict who had his sights set on writing a
novel ever since leaving university. The book took him five years to
write, whilst teaching day and evening classes as a college lecturer.

"Amazing powers of imagination and
storytelling."

"Emotive, sometimes shocking; delightfully
full of suspense."

"A real page-turner, a wonderful adventure
in a world with similarities to Orwell's 1984."

"A dramatic ending and a fantastic book."

"Exciting, challenging, thought-provoking."

How could such a creature as a whale have truly existed?

Very few people in this society of slaves and informers have
ever seen the awe-inspiring waves…
    … until a new punishment is instituted at Turret Rock.

Hermanus loves the sea and is plunged into the unexpected
constraints and realisations of the life he has always wanted;
will he then risk being persuaded that the whales really did
exist – or are they just an imaginative story from the past?

Truth or myths? A multi-faceted dilemma of loyalties.

Searching for his brother,
        the culture shock of a new life;
                how old do you have to be for freedom?

Also published by Fygleaves: New authors revealing their leaves to the world

ENVELOPE OF A LETTER

BY LAURA DAWN

An author who came to prominence in our 2004 short story competition with her entry Whitewash. Laura finished writing this novel while working in a bookshop in her native Essex, and it was published in 2005 when she was only 19.

"All the romantic appeal of the Pride and Prejudice era, wonderfully told for a contemporary reader through the eyes of a post-modern narrator."

"A fabulous period book, with plenty of laughs along the way."

"Combines the tragic with the light-hearted in a romantic comedy that 'goes deeper'."

"A rollercoaster of emotions."

An invitation that cannot be refused?

When two teenage sisters experience a carriage accident they are each left with diametrically opposed ambitions: Anna to enjoy the blossoming Regency society to the utmost; Annette to shun the world and hide her physical scars.

Only letters offer Annette the opportunity of a relationship unconditioned by her disfigured appearance, and as a result of her correspondence she finds herself invited to visit the charming and accomplished Clemence Skye at his opulent castle: the sisters hatch a plan which soon spirals rapidly out of control...

A dazzling array of twists, and a plot full of characters destined for the romance and tragedy which the sisters provoke.

You can support new authors revealing their leaves to the world.

Fygleaves exists to provide opportunities for new writers: many of the writers featured in this book are previously unpublished. Publishing is becoming a harder and harder world to break into, unless you are already famous for something else!

But it is consumer choice which makes the world the way it is. We might bemoan the demise of the corner shop but we all contribute to the problem by shopping in the supermarket.

Consumer power carries a great weight, if it can be harnessed: the rise in Fair Trade goods would not have been possible if it wasn't for everyday customers lobbying their local supermarket to stock them. For this reason Fygleaves is starting its own initiative to create a market for previously unpublished authors.

Although we are still bound by the need to accept only those manuscripts which we consider to have the quality and enough appeal to interest general fiction readers, we exist to publish novels by writers who have never been given their opportunity before: in this way we aim to be a springboard for talented authors reaching for bigger things.

And that is where we need pioneer readers – readers who are willing to buy and read the books we publish even if they do not have broad media coverage or exposure in the press.

If you are interested in finding out more, and if you are willing to consider becoming a pioneer reader, visit us at www.pioneer-readers.org and you too can help change the publishing world.

Interested in our next competition?

Full details of our annual competition are available on our website
**www.5photostory.com**

Want to give feedback to our judge or the short story writers?

We welcome constructive comments about all the short stories included in this book, and invite you to share your feedback about these stories, or any other aspect of Fygleaves Publishing's work, on our discussion board online at www.fygleaves.co.uk/discussionboard/index.php